She was pregnant. Very pregnant.

He had a million questions and didn't have time to nail down a single one before Rita threw herself into his arms.

"Jack!" She hugged him hard, then seemed to notice he wasn't returning her hug, so she let him go and stepped back. Confusion filled her eyes even as her smile faded into a flat, thin line. "How can you be here? I thought you must be dead. I never heard from you and—"

"Not here," he ground out, giving himself points for keeping a tight rein on the emotions rushing through him. "Let's take a walk."

"I'm working," she pointed out, waving her hand at the counter and customers behind her.

"Take a break." He needed some answers and he wasn't going to be denied. She was here. She was pregnant. Judging by the size of her belly, he was guessing about six months pregnant. That meant they had to talk. Now.

Little Secrets:
His Unexpected Heir

MAUREEN CHILD

First published in Great Britain 2017
By Mills & Boon, an imprint of HarperCollins*Publishers*
1 London Bridge Street, London, SE1 9GF

Large Print edition 2017

© 2017 Maureen Child

ISBN: 978-0-263-07214-3

Printed and bound in Great Britain
by CPI Antony Rowe, Chippenham, Wiltshire

Maureen Child writes for the Mills & Boon Desire line and can't imagine a better job. A seven-time finalist for a prestigious Romance Writers of America RITA® Award, Maureen is an author of more than one hundred romance novels. Her books regularly appear on bestseller lists and have won several awards, including a Prism Award, a National Readers' Choice Award, a Colorado Romance Writers Award of Excellence and a Golden Quill Award. She is a native Californian but has recently moved to the mountains of Utah.

To my mom, Sallye Carberry,
because she loves romance novels
and shared that love with me.

One

Jack Buchanan listened to his interior decorator talk about swatches and color and found his mind drifting...to *anything* else.

Four months ago, he'd been in a desert, making life-and-death decisions. Today, he was in an upholstery shop in Long Beach, California, deciding between leather or fabric for the bar seats on the Buchanan Company's latest cruise ship. He didn't know whether to be depressed or amused. So he went with impatient.

"Which fabric will hold up better?" he asked,

cutting into the argument between the decorator and the upholsterer.

"The leather," they both said at once, turning to look at him.

"Then use the fabric." Jack pointed at a bolt of midnight blue cloth shot through with silver threads. "We're building a fantasy bar. I'm less interested in wear and more concerned with the look of the place. If you want black leather in the mix, too, use it on the booth seats."

While the decorator and the upholsterer instantly jumped on that idea and put their heads together to plan, Jack shifted his gaze to encompass the shop. Family-owned, Dan Black and his sons, Mark and Tom, ran the place and did great work. Jack had seen that much for himself.

The shop itself was long and wide and filled with not only barstools, but also couches, chairs and tables being refinished. A chemical scent hung in the air as two men at the back of the room worked on projects. The low-pitched roar of an industrial sewing machine was like white noise in the background and the guy seated at it moved quickly, efficiently. Their work was fast and good enough that they'd also done jobs for the navy and Jack figured if they could handle *that*, they could handle his cruise ship.

But why the hell was Jack even here? He was the CEO of Buchanan Shipping. Didn't he have minions he could have sent to take care of this?

But even as he thought it, he reminded himself that being here today, in person, had all been his idea. To immerse himself in every aspect of the business. He'd been away for the last *ten* years, so he had a lot of catching up to do.

Jack, his brother, Sam, and their sister, Cass, had all interned at Buchanan growing up. They'd put in their time from the ground up, starting in janitorial, since their father had firmly believed that kids raised with all the money in the world grew up to be asses.

He'd made sure that *his* children knew what it was to really work. To be alongside employees who would expect them to do the job and who had the ability to fire them if they didn't. Thomas Buchanan raised his kids to respect those who worked for them and to always remember that without those employees, they wouldn't have a business. So Jack, Sam and Cass had worked their way through every level at the company. They'd had to buy their own cars, pay for their own insurance and if they wanted designer clothes, they had to save up for them.

Now, looking back, Jack could see it had been the right thing to do. At the time, he hadn't loved it of course. But today, he could step into the CEO's shoes with a lot less trepidation because of his father's rules. He had the basics on running the company. But it was this stuff—the day-to-day, small but necessary decisions—that he had to get used to.

Buchanan Shipping had interests all over the world. From cruise liners to cargo ships to the fishing fleet Jack's brother, Sam, ran out of San Diego. The company had grown well beyond his great-grandfather's dreams when he'd started the business with one commercial fishing boat.

The Buchanans had been on the California coast since before the gold rush. While other men bought land and fought with the dirt to scratch out a fortune, the Buchanans had turned to the sea. They had a reputation for excellence that nothing had ever marred and Jack wanted to keep it that way.

Their latest cruise ship was top-of-the-line, state-of-the-art throughout and would, he told himself, more than live up to her name, *The Sea Queen.*

"Mr. Buchanan," the decorator said, forcing Jack out of his thoughts and back to reality.

"Yeah. What is it?"

"There are still choices to be made on height of stools, width of booths…"

Okay, details were one thing, minutiae were another.

Jack stopped her with one hand held up for silence. "You can handle that, Ms. Price." To take any sting out of his words, he added, "I trust your judgment," and watched pleasure flash in her eyes.

"Of course, of course," she said. "I'll fax you

a complete record of all decisions made this afternoon."

"That's fine. Thanks." He shook hands with Daniel Black, waved a hand at the men in the back of the shop and left. Stepping outside, he was immediately slapped by a strong, cold breeze that carried the scent of the sea. The sky was a clear, bold blue and this small corner of the city hummed with an energy that pulsed inside Jack.

He wasn't ready to go back to the company. To sit in that palatial office, fielding phone calls and going over reports. Being outside, even being here, dealing with fabrics of all things, was better than being stuck behind his desk. With that thought firmly in mind, he walked to his car, got in and fired it up. Steering away from work, responsibility and the restless, itchy feeling scratching at his soul, Jack drove toward peace.

Okay, maybe *peace* was the wrong word, he told himself twenty minutes later. The crowd on Main Street in Seal Beach was thick, the noise deafening and the mingled scents from restaurants, pubs and bakeries swamped him.

Jack Buchanan fought his way through the summer crowds blocking the sidewalk. He'd been home from his last tour of duty for four months and he still wasn't used to being surrounded by so many people. Made him feel on edge, as if every nerve in his body was strung tight enough to snap.

Frowning at the thought, he sidestepped a couple of women who had stopped in the middle of the sidewalk to argue about a pair of shoes, for God's sake. Shaking his head, he walked a little faster, dodging gawking tourists, teenagers with surfboards and kids racing in and out of the crowd, peals of laughter hanging in their wake.

Summer in Southern California was always going to be packed with the tourists who flocked in from all over the world. And ordinarily Jack avoided the worst of the crowds by keeping close to his office building and the penthouse apartment he lived in. But at least once a month, Jack forced himself to go out into the throngs of people—just to prove to himself that he could.

Being surrounded by people brought out every

defensive instinct he possessed. He felt on guard, watching the passing people through suspicious, wary eyes and hated himself for it. But four months home from a battlefield wasn't long enough to ease the instincts that had kept him alive in the desert. And still, he worked at forcing himself to relax those instincts because he refused to be defined by what he'd gone through. What he'd seen.

A small boy bulleted around a corner and slammed right into Jack. Every muscle in Jack's body tensed until he deliberately relaxed, caught the kid by the shoulders to keep him from falling and said, "You should watch where you're running."

"Sorry, mister." The kid jerked his head back, swinging his long blond hair out of his eyes.

"It's okay," Jack said, releasing both the boy and the sharp jolt of adrenaline still pumping inside him. "Just watch it."

"Right. Gotta go." The boy took off, headed for the beach and the pier at the end of the street.

Jack remembered, vaguely, what it had been

like to be ten years old with a world of summer stretched out ahead of you. With the sun beating down on him and a sea breeze dancing past, Jack could almost recapture the sensation of complete freedom that everyone lost as they grew up. Frowning at his own thoughts, he concentrated again on the crowd and realized it had been a couple of months since he'd been in Seal Beach.

A small beach community, it lay alongside Long Beach where he lived and worked, but Jack didn't make a habit of coming here. Memories were thick and he tended to avoid them, because remembering wouldn't get him a damn thing. But against his will, images filled his mind.

Last December, he'd been on R and R. He'd had two weeks to return to his life, see his family and decompress. He'd spent the first few days visiting his father, brother and sister, then he'd drawn back, pulling into himself. He'd come to the beach then, walking the sand at night, letting the sea whisper to him. Until the night he'd met *her.*

A beautiful woman, alone on the beach, the

moonlight caressing her skin, shining in her hair until he'd almost convinced himself she wasn't real. Until she turned her head and gave him a cautious smile.

She should have been cautious. A woman alone on a dark beach. Rita Marchetti had been smart enough to be careful and strong enough to be friendly. They'd talked, he remembered, there in the moonlight and then met again the following day and the day after that. The remainder of his leave, he'd spent with her, and every damn moment of that time was etched into his brain in living, vibrant color. He could hear the sound of her voice. The music of her laughter. He saw the shine in her eyes and felt the silk of her touch.

"And you've been working for months to forget it," he reminded himself in a mutter. "No point in dredging it up now."

What they'd found together all those months ago was over now. There was no going back. He'd made a promise to himself. One he intended to keep. Never again would he put himself in the position of loss and pain and he wouldn't ever be close enough to someone else that *his* loss would bring pain.

It was a hard lesson to learn, but he had learned it in the hot, dry sands of a distant country. And that lesson haunted him to this day. Enough that just walking through this crowd made him edgy. There was an itch at the back of his neck and it took everything he had not to give in to the urge to get out. Get away.

But Jack Buchanan didn't surrender to the dregs of fear, so he kept walking, made himself notice the everyday world pulsing around him. Along the street, a pair of musicians were playing for the crowd and the dollar bills tossed into an open guitar case. Shop owners had tables set up outside their storefronts to entice customers and farther down the street, a line snaked from a bakery's doors all along the sidewalk.

He hadn't been downtown in months, so he'd never seen the bakery before. Apparently, though, it had quite the loyal customer base. Dozens of people—from teenagers to career men and women waited patiently to get through the open bakery door. As he got closer, amazing scents wafted through the air and he understood the crowds gathering. Idly, Jack glanced through the wide, shining front window at the throng within, then stopped dead as an all too familiar laugh drifted to him.

Everything inside Jack went cold and still. He hadn't heard that laughter in months, but he'd have known it anywhere. Throaty, rich, it made him think of long, hot nights, silk sheets and big brown eyes staring up into his in the darkness.

He'd tried to forget her. Had, he'd thought, buried the memories; yet now, they came roaring back, swamping him until Jack had to fight for breath.

Even as he told himself it couldn't be her, Jack was bypassing the line and stalking into the bakery. He followed the sound of that laugh as if it were a trail of breadcrumbs. He had to know. Had to see.

"Hey, dude," a surfer with long dark hair told him, "end of the line's back a ways."

"I'm not buying anything," he growled out and

sent the younger man a look icy enough to freeze blood. Must have worked because the guy went quiet and gave a half shrug.

But Jack had already moved on. He was moving through the scattering of tables and chairs, sliding through the throng of people clustered in front of a wide, tall glass display case. Conversations rose and fell all around him. The cheerful jingle of the old-fashioned cash register sounded out every purchase as if celebrating. But Jack wasn't paying attention. His sharp gaze swept across the people in the shop, looking for the woman he'd never thought to see again.

Then that laugh came again and he spun around like a wolf finding the scent of its mate. Gaze narrowed, heartbeat thundering in his ears, he spotted her—and everything else in the room dropped away.

Rita Marchetti. He took a breath and simply stared at her for what felt like forever. Her smile was wide and bright, her gaze focused on customers who laughed with her. What the hell was she doing in a bakery in Seal Beach, California, when she lived in Ogden, Utah? And why did she have to look so damn good?

He watched her, smiling and laughing with a customer as she boxed what looked like a couple dozen cookies, then deftly tied a white ribbon around the tall red box. Her hands were small and efficient. Her eyes were big and brown and shone with warmth. Her shoulder-length curly brown hair was pulled into a ponytail at the base of her neck and swung like a pendulum with her every movement.

Her skin was golden—all over, as he had reason to know—her mouth was wide and full, and though she was short, her figure was lush. His memories were clear enough that every drop of blood in his body dropped to his groin, leaving him light-headed…briefly. In an instant, though, all of that changed and a surge of differing emotions raced through him. Pleasure at seeing her again, anger at being faced with a past he'd already let go of and desire that was so hot, so thick, it grabbed him by the throat and choked off his air.

The heat of his gaze must have alerted her. She looked up and across the crowd, locking her gaze with his. Her eyes went wide, her amazing mouth dropped open and she lifted one hand to the base of her throat as if she, too, was having trouble breathing. Gaze still locked with his, she walked away from the counter, came around the display case and though Jack braced himself for facing her again—nothing could have prepared him for what he saw next.

She was pregnant.

Very pregnant.

Her belly was big, rounded and covered by a skintight, bright yellow T-shirt. The hem of her white capris ended just below her knees and she wore slip-on sneakers in a yellow bright enough to match her shirt.

He saw and noted all of that in a split second before he focused again on her rounded belly. Jack's heartbeat galloped in his chest as he lifted his eyes to meet hers. He had a million questions and didn't have time to nail down a single one before, in spite of the crowd watching them, Rita threw herself into his arms.

"Jack!" She hugged him hard, then seemed to notice he wasn't returning her hug, so she let him go and stepped back. Confusion filled her eyes even as her smile faded into a flat, thin line. "How can you be here? I thought you must be dead. I never heard from you and—"

He flinched and gave a quick glance around. Their little reunion was garnering way too much attention. No way was he going to have this chat with an audience listening to every word. And, he told himself, gaze dropping to that belly again, they had a *lot* to talk about.

"Not here," he ground out, giving himself points for keeping a tight rein on the emotions rushing through him. "Let's take a walk."

"I'm working," she pointed out, waving her hand at the counter and customers behind her.

"Take a break." Jack felt everyone watching them and an itch at the back of his neck urged him to get moving. But he was going nowhere without Rita. He needed some answers and he wasn't going to be denied. She was *here*. She was *pregnant*. Judging by the size of her belly, he was guessing about six months pregnant. That meant they had to talk. Now.

She frowned a little and even the downturn of her mouth was sexy. Which told Jack he was walking into some serious trouble. But there was no way to avoid any of it.

While he stared at her, he could practically see the wheels turning in her brain. She didn't like him telling her what to do, but she was so surprised to see him that she clearly wanted answers as badly as he did. She was smart, opinionated and had a temper, he recalled, that could blister paint. Just a few of the reasons that he'd once been crazy about her.

Coming to a decision, Rita called out, "Casey," and a cute redhead behind the counter looked up. "I'm taking a break. Back in fifteen."

"Right, boss," the woman said and went right back to ringing up the latest customer.

"Might take more than fifteen," he warned her even as she started past him toward the door.

"No, it won't," she said over her shoulder.

Whatever her original response to seeing him had been, she was cool and calm now, having no doubt figured out that he deliberately hadn't contacted her when he got home. They'd talk about that, too. But not here.

People were watching. The redhead looked curious, but Jack didn't give a damn. He caught up with Rita in two steps, took hold of her upper arm and steered her past the crowd and out the door. Once they were clear of the shop, though, Rita pulled free of his grip. "I can walk on my own, Jack."

Without another word, she proved it, heading down the block toward the Seal Beach pier. The tree-lined street offered patches of shade and she moved from sunlight to shadow, her strides short, but sure.

He watched her for a couple of minutes, just to enjoy the view. She'd always had a world-class butt and damned if it wasn't good to see it again. He'd forgotten how little she was. Not delicate, he told himself. Not by a long shot. The woman was fierce, which he liked and her temper was truly something to behold. But right now, it was his own temper he had to deal with. Why was she here? Why was she *pregnant*? And why the hell hadn't he known about it?

His long legs covered the distance between them quickly, then he matched his stride to hers until they were stopped at a red light at Ocean Avenue. Across the street lay the beach, the ocean and the pier. Even from a distance, Jack could see surfers riding waves, fishermen dotting the pier and cyclists racing along the sidewalk.

While they waited for the light to change, he looked down at her, and inevitably, his gaze was drawn to the mound of her belly. His own insides jumped then fisted. Shoving one hand through his hair, he told himself he should have written to her as he'd said he would. Should have contacted her when he came home for good. But he'd been in a place where he hadn't wanted to see anyone. Talk to anyone. Hell, even his family hadn't been able to reach him.

"How long have you been home?" she asked, her voice nearly lost beneath the hum of traffic.

"Four months."

She looked up at him and he read anger and sorrow, mingled into a dark mess that dimmed the golden light in those dark brown eyes. "Good to know."

Before he could speak again the light changed and she stepped off the curb. Once again he took her arm and when she would have shaken him off, he firmly held on.

Once they crossed the street, she pulled away and he let her go, following after her as she stalked toward a small green park at the edge of a parking lot. Just beyond was a kids' playground, and beside that, the pier that snaked out into the sea.

The wind whipped her ponytail and tugged at the edges of his suit jacket. She turned to look up at him and when she spoke, he heard both pain and temper in her voice.

"I thought you were dead."

"Rita—"

"No." She shook her head and held up one

hand to keep him silent. "You *let* me think it," she accused. "You told me you'd write to me. You didn't. You've been home four months and never looked for me."

Jack blew out a breath. "No, I didn't."

She rocked back on her heels as if he'd struck her. "Wow. You're not even sorry, are you?"

His gaze fixed on hers. "No, I'm not. There are reasons for what I did."

She folded her arms across her chest, unconsciously drawing his attention to her belly again. "Can't wait to hear them."

Two

Rita was shaking.

Her hands clenched, she tried to ease her galloping heartbeat and steady her breathing. But just standing beside Jack Buchanan made that almost impossible. She slid a glance at him from beneath lowered lashes and her breath caught. Even in profile, he was almost too gorgeous. That black hair, longer now than it had been when they met, those ice-blue eyes, strong jaw, firm mouth, all came together until a knot of emotion settled in her throat, nearly choking her.

For one magical week six months ago, she had

been in love and she'd thought he felt the same. Then he was gone, and she was alone, waiting for a letter that never came. So the last several months, Rita had been convinced he was dead. Killed in service on his last tour of duty. When they met, she knew he was a Marine on R and R. Knew that he would be returning to danger. But somehow, she'd convinced herself that he would be safe. That he would come back. To her.

He'd promised to write and when she didn't hear from him, Rita had mourned him. She'd had to face the stark, shattering truth that he was never coming home again. That he'd made the ultimate sacrifice and everything they'd found together so briefly was over.

And now, he was *here*.

"How did you find me?"

He shook his head. "I didn't. I was just walking down the street. Heard your laugh and it stopped me cold."

Oh, God. Just an accident. A whim of Fate. He hadn't been looking for her. Had probably forgotten all about her the moment he left her six months ago. And what had she done? *Mourned.*

Grieved. The memory of that pain fueled her next words.

"I thought you were dead," she finally said, and hoped he couldn't hear the pain in her voice.

He took a breath, blew it out and said, "I wanted you to."

Another blow and this one had her reeling. He'd *wanted* her to mourn him? To go through the pain of a loss so deeply felt that it had been weeks before she'd even been able to *function*? The only thing that had kept her going, that had gotten her out of bed in the mornings, was her baby. Knowing that Jack had left her with this gift, this child, had given her strength. She'd gone on, telling herself that Jack would want her to.

Now she finds out he *wanted* her to believe he was dead?

"Who are you?" she asked, shaking her head and blinking furiously to keep tears she wouldn't show him at bay.

"The same guy you used to know," he ground out.

"No." She stiffened her spine, lifted her chin

and glared at him. "The Jack I knew would never have put me through the last six months."

For an instant, she thought she saw shame flash across his eyes, but it was gone as quickly as it had appeared, so Rita put it down to wishful thinking.

"This isn't about me," he said quietly and she heard the tight control in his voice. "You're pregnant."

"Very observant." God. She wrapped her arms around her belly protectively.

"How far along?"

Shocked, Rita bit back the words that first flew to her mouth. Temper spiked, and she had to wrestle it into submission. She knew what he was asking—*who's the father?* And she didn't know if she was more hurt than angry or if it was a tie between the two.

"Six months," she said pointedly. "So your cleverly veiled question is answered. You're the father."

Not that she was happy about that at the moment. She loved her baby, *had* loved its father.

But this stranger looking down at her through icy cold eyes was someone she didn't even recognize.

"And you didn't tell me about it."

Before she could stop it, a short, sharp laugh shot from her throat. Shaking her head in complete wonder at his ridiculous statement, she countered, "How was I supposed to do that, Jack? I had no way of contacting you. You were going to write to me with your address."

A muscle in his jaw twitched and his eyes narrowed, but she didn't care.

"I don't think sending a letter addressed to Jack Buchanan, United States Marine Corps, somewhere in a desert would have found you."

"Fine. I get it." He pushed the edges of his jacket back and stuffed his hands into his pockets. The wind lifted his dark red power tie, turning it into a waving flag. His hair was ruffled, his eyes were cold and his jaw tight. "Like I said, there were reasons."

"Still haven't heard them."

"Yeah. Not important right now. What is important," he said, his gaze shifting to the mound of her belly and back up to her eyes again, "is my baby."

"You mean *my* baby," she corrected and instantly wished she hadn't come to work that day. If she'd taken the day off, she wouldn't have been in the bakery when he walked by and none of this would be happening.

"Rita, if you think I'm walking away from this, you're wrong."

"Why wouldn't I think that?" she argued, moving away from him, instinctively keeping a safe distance between him and her child. "You walked away before. Never looked back."

"That's not true," he muttered, letting his gaze slide from hers to focus on the ocean instead. "I thought about you."

Her heart twisted, but Rita wouldn't allow herself to be swayed. He'd walked away. Shut her out. Let her *mourn* him, for heaven's sake. *I thought about you* just didn't make up for the misery she'd lived through.

"And I should believe you?"

He slanted her a glance. "Believe or not, it changes nothing."

"That much is true anyway," Rita agreed. "Look, I have to get back to work."

"Your boss won't fire you if you take more than fifteen minutes."

She laughed a little, but there was no warmth in it. "I *am* the boss. It's my bakery and I have to get back to it."

"Yours?"

"Yeah," she said, turning away to head back up Main Street.

"Why did you come here?" he asked and had her pausing to look over her shoulder at him. "I mean, *here*, Seal Beach. You lived in Utah when we met."

Rita stared at him and whether she wanted to admit it to herself or not, there was a jolt of need inside her she couldn't quite ignore. With the sun pouring down on him, he looked both dangerous and appealing. He was tall and broad-shouldered and even in an elegant suit, he looked…intimidating. Was it any wonder why she'd fallen so hard for him?

That was then, she reminded herself; this was now.

"I moved here because I wanted to feel closer to you," she admitted, then added, "of course, that's when I thought you were dead. Now, the only thing that's dead is what I felt for you."

When she walked away, Rita felt his gaze fix on her. And she knew this wouldn't be the last time she'd see him.

And that was both worrying and comforting.

That afternoon, Jack went back to the bakery, took a table that allowed him to keep his back to a wall and ordered coffee. A seemingly never-ending stream of customers came and went, laughed, chatted and walked out with red bakery boxes. This was her place, Jack thought with admiration. The shop was small but it had an old-world elegance to it.

Gleaming wood floors, dark blue granite counters, brass-and-chrome cash register, glistening glass display cases boasting pastries and cookies. There were brass sconces on the walls and pots of flowers and trailing greenery in strategic spots. It looked, he thought, just as she wanted it to. Like an exclusive Italian shop.

His gaze tracked her employees as they hustled to serve their customers, then shifted to land on Rita herself. She was still ignoring him, but he didn't mind. Gave him time to think.

Jack's mind was still buzzing. Not only at news of the baby but at seeing Rita again. He'd worked for months to wipe her out of his memories and now everything came rushing back in a tidal wave of images.

He saw her standing at the water's edge, moonlight spearing down on her from a cold, black sky. December at the beach was cold and she was wearing a jacket, but she was holding her shoes in one hand and letting the icy water lick at her toes.

Her hair was a tangle of dark brown curls that lifted and swirled around her head in the ever-present wind. She heard him approaching and in-

stantly turned her head to look at him. He should have walked on, cut away from her and headed for the pier, but something about her made him stop. He kept a safe distance between them because he didn't want to worry her, but as he looked into her big brown eyes, he felt drawn to her like nothing he'd ever experienced before.

"Don't be scared," he said. "I'm harmless."

She smiled faintly and tipped her head to one side. "Oh, I doubt that. But I'm not scared."

"Why not?" he asked, tucking his hands into the pockets of his jeans. "Empty beach, in the dark, strange guy..."

"You don't seem so strange. Plus, I'm pretty tough," she said. "And I run really fast."

He laughed, admiring the way she stood there, so calm and self-assured. "Noted."

"So," she said, "I'm a tourist. What's your excuse for being at the beach when it's this cold?"

Jack turned to look out over the spread of black water dotted with white froth as it tumbled toward shore. "I've been away for a while, so I want to appreciate this view."

"You're in the military?" she asked.

He glanced at her and smiled. "That obvious?"

"It's the haircut," she admitted, smiling.

"Yeah," he scrubbed one hand across the top of his head. "Hard to disguise I guess. Marines."

She smiled and he thought she was the most beautiful woman he'd ever seen.

"Well, thank you for your service," she said, then added, "do you get tired of people saying that?"

"Nope," he assured her. "That never gets old. So, a tourist. From where?"

"Utah," she said, smiling. "Ogden, specifically."

"It's pretty," he said. "Though it's been a few years since I've been there."

Her smile brightened, nearly blinding him with the power of it. "Thanks, it is gorgeous, and I love the mountains. Especially in fall. But—" she half turned, letting her gaze slide across the ocean "—this is hard to resist."

"Yeah, I've missed it."

"I bet," she said, tipping her head to one side to look at him. "How long have you been gone?"

He shrugged, not really wanting to bring the desert heat and the memory of gunfire into this moment. "Too long."

As if she understood what he wasn't saying, she only nodded and they fell into silence until the only sound was the pulse and beat of the sea as it surged toward shore only to rush back out again.

At last, though, she reached up to push her hair back out of her face, smiled again and said, "I should be getting back to the hotel. It was nice meeting you."

"But we didn't," he interrupted quickly, suddenly desperate to keep her from leaving. "Meet, I mean. I'm Jack."

"Rita."

"I like it."

"Thanks."

"Do you really have to get back, or could I buy you a cup of coffee?"

She studied him for a long minute or two, then nodded. "I'd like that, Jack."

"I'm glad, but you sure are trusting."

"Actually," she said quietly, "I'm really not. But for some reason..."

"Yeah," he answered. "There's something..."

He walked toward her and held out one hand. She took it and the instant he touched her, he felt a hot buzz of something bright, staggering. He looked down at their joined hands, then closed his fingers around hers. "Come with me, Rita. I know just the place."

"Excuse me."

The tone of those words told Jack that it wasn't the first time the woman standing beside his table had said them. It was the redhead. "I'm sorry, what?"

"Rita says to tell you this is on the house," she said, setting a plate with two cannoli on it in front of him.

He frowned a little.

"Yeah, she told me you wouldn't look happy about it," the woman said. "I'm Casey. Can I get you more coffee?"

"Sure, thanks." She picked up his cup and walked to the counter, but Jack stopped paying attention almost immediately. Instead, his gaze sought out Rita.

As if she was expecting it, she turned to meet his stare and even from across that crowded room, it felt to Jack as it had that first night. As if they were alone on a deserted beach.

Well, damn it.

Casey was back an instant later with a fresh cup of coffee. Never taking his eyes off Rita, Jack leaned against the wall behind him and slowly sipped at his coffee. They had a lot to talk about. Too bad it wasn't *talking* on his mind.

A couple of hours later, the customers were gone and Rita was closing up. He'd already seen the sign that advertised their hours—open at seven, closed at six. Now as twilight settled on the beach, he watched Rita turn the deadbolt and flip the closed sign. Jack had had enough coffee to float one of his cargo ships and he'd had far too long to sit by himself and watch as she moved through the life she'd built since he'd last seen her.

"Why did you stay here all day, Jack?" She walked toward him. "This is borderline stalking."

"Not stalking. Sitting. Eating cannoli."

Her lips twitched and he found himself hoping she might show him that wide smile that he'd seen the first night they met. But it didn't come, so he let it go.

"Should you be on your feet this much?" he blurted.

Both of her eyebrows lifted as she set both fists on her hips. "Really?"

"It's a reasonable question," he insisted. "You're pregnant."

Now her big brown eyes went wide with feigned surprise. "I am?"

Jack sighed at the ridiculousness of the conversation. "Funny. Look, I just found out about this, so you could cut me some slack."

She took the chair opposite him, sitting down with a sigh of relief. "Why should I? It's not my fault you didn't know about the baby. You could have been a part of this from the beginning, Jack, if you had written to me." She reached over and plucked a dry leaf off the closest potted plant. Then she looked at him again. "But you didn't. Instead, you disappeared and let me think you were dead."

Yeah, he could see this from her side, and he didn't much care for the view. But that didn't change the fact that he'd done what he thought was necessary at the time. He'd had to put her out of his mind to survive when he went back to his duty station. Thoughts of her hadn't had any place in that hot, sandy miserable piece of ground and keeping her in his mind only threatened the concentration he needed to keep himself and his men alive.

Sure, at first, he'd thought that having her to think about would get him through, remind him that there was another world outside the desperate one he was caught up in. But two weeks after returning to deployment, something had happened to convince him that images of home were only a distraction. That keeping her face in his mind was dangerous.

So, he'd pushed the memories into a dark, deep

corner of his brain and closed a door on them. It hadn't been easy, but he'd been convinced that it was the right thing to do.

Now he wasn't so sure.

"Why?" she asked, folding her hands on top of the small round glass-topped table. "You could at least tell me that much. Why did you never write, Jack?"

His gaze locked on hers. "It really doesn't matter now, does it? It's done. We have to deal with *now*."

Shaking her head, Rita sat back in the chair, and tapped the fingers of her right hand against the tabletop. "There is no *we*, Jack. Not anymore."

Beside him, a wide window overlooked Main Street. Late afternoon sunlight shone on the sidewalks, illuminating the people strolling through the early evening cool. It looked so normal. So peaceful. Yet seeing even that small crowd of pedestrians had Jack's insides going on alert. He didn't like the fact that he couldn't really relax around a lot of people anymore, but he had to accept that fact. So he turned away from strangers to look at a woman he'd once known so well.

"As long as there's a baby, there's a *we*," he told her. "If you think I'm going to walk away from my own kid, you're wrong."

Instinctively, she dropped her hands to the curve of her belly and he realized she made that move a lot. Was it something all women did, or was Rita feeling threatened by seeing him again?

"Jack—"

"We can talk about it, work it out together," he said, interrupting her to make sure she understood where he was on this. "But bottom line, I'm here now. You're going to have to deal with it."

"You don't get to give me orders, Jack." She gave him a sad smile. "I live my own life. I run my own business. I raise my own child."

"And mine."

"Since your half and mine are intertwined," she quipped, "yes."

"Not acceptable." And this conversation was veering into the repetitive. It was getting him nowhere fast and he could see the flash of stubborn determination in her eyes that told him she wasn't going to budge. Well, hell. He could out-stubborn anyone.

"I really think you should go, Jack." She stood up, rubbing her belly idly with one hand.

He followed that motion and felt his heart trip-hammer in his chest. His child. Inside the woman that had been his so briefly. Damned if he'd leave. Walk away. It probably would have been better for all of them, but he wouldn't be doing it.

"I'll take you home," he said, standing to look down at her.

She chuckled. "I am home. I live in the apartment upstairs."

"You're kidding." He frowned, glanced at the ceiling as if he could see through the barrier into what had to be a very small apartment. "You live over a bakery."

She stiffened at the implied insult. "It's convenient. I get up at four every morning to start the baking, so all I have to do is walk downstairs."

"You're not raising my kid above a bakery."

When her eyes flashed and one dark eyebrow

winged up, he knew he'd stepped wrong. But it didn't matter how he'd said it if the end was the same. His kid was not going to live above a bakery. Period.

"And, the circle is complete," she said, walking to the front door. She unlocked it, opened it wide and waved one hand as if scooping him out the door. "I want you to leave, Jack."

"All right." He conceded on this point. For now. He started past her, then stopped when their bodies were just a breath apart. When he caught her scent and could almost feel the heat shimmering off her body. Everything in him twisted tight and squeezed. Giving in to the urge driving him, he reached out, took her chin in his hand and tipped her face up until her eyes were locked with his. "This isn't over, Rita. It's just getting started."

Sitting on her couch in her—all right, yes, tiny apartment—Rita curled her feet underneath her as her fingers tightened on her cellphone. "What am I supposed to do, Gina?"

Instead of answering, her sister called out, "Ally, do *not* pour milk on the dog again."

"But *why*?" A young, loud voice shouted in response.

In spite of everything going on in her life at the moment, Rita grinned. Ally was two years old with a hard head, a stubborn streak a mile wide and a sweet smile that usually got her out of trouble.

"Because he doesn't like it!" Gina huffed out a breath, came back on the line, and whispered, "Actually he *does* like it, idiot dog. Then he spends all night licking the milk off himself, my floor is sticky and he smells like sour milk."

It was times like these that Rita really missed her family. Her parents. Her sister. Her two older brothers. All of her nieces and nephews. They were all in Ogden, working at the family bakery, Marchetti's. Rita's family was loud, boisterous, argumentative and sometimes she missed them so much she actually *ached* to be with them.

Like now, for instance.

"Michael and Braden Franco!" Gina shouted.

"If you ride your skateboards down the steps and one of you breaks another bone, I will burn those boards in the fire pit—"

The five-year-old twins were adventurous and barely containable. It's what Rita loved best about them.

Gina broke off with a satisfied sigh. "Another crisis averted. Sorry sweetie, what were you saying again?"

Back to the matter at hand. "Jack. He's alive. He's *here*." Rita bit down hard on her bottom lip and blinked wildly to keep the tears filling her eyes from falling. Though there was no one there to see her cry, she didn't want to give Jack the satisfaction.

Hadn't she already cried rivers for Jack? After two months had passed without a word from him, Rita had known that he was gone, no doubt killed in action somewhere far away. What other reason, she'd told herself, could there have been for him not to write her?

They'd had such an amazing connection. Something strong and powerful had grown between them in one short week. She'd loved him fiercely even after so short a time. But then her mother had always told her that time had nothing to do with love. If you knew someone five days or five years, the feelings didn't change.

It had taken Rita much less than five days to know that Jack was the one man she wanted. Then he was gone and the pain of loss had crippled her. Until she'd discovered she was pregnant.

"He's *there*?" Gina whispered as if somehow Jack could overhear her. "At your apartment?"

"No," she said, though she tossed a quick look toward the door at the back of the building that opened onto a staircase leading to a small parking lot. She half expected Jack to show up on her landing and knock. Shaking her head, she said, "No, he's not here, here. He's here in Seal Beach. He came into the bakery today."

"Oh. My. God." A moment or two passed before Gina continued. "What did you do? What did he say? Where the hell has he been? Why didn't he write to you? Bastard."

A short laugh shot from Rita's throat. She heard

the outrage in her sister's voice and was grateful for it. How did anyone survive without a sister?

"I nearly shrieked when I saw him," Rita confessed. "Then I hugged him, damn it."

"Of course you hugged him," Gina soothed. "Then did you kick him?"

She laughed again. "No, but I wish I'd thought of it at the time."

"Well, if you need me, Jimmy can watch the kids for a few days. I'll fly out there and kick him for you."

Rita sighed and smiled all at once. "I can always count on you, Gina."

"Of course you can. So where's he been?"

"I don't know."

"Why didn't he write?"

Rita frowned. "I don't know."

"Well, what did he say?"

Rita picked up her cup of herbal tea and took a sip. "He only wanted to talk about the baby."

"Oh, boy."

"Exactly." Sighing more heavily now, Rita set the cup down on the coffee table again. "He was…surprised to find out I was pregnant and he didn't look happy about it."

"We don't need him to be happy. But why wouldn't he be? Who doesn't like babies? Hold on. I'll be right back."

While she waited, Rita's head dropped back against the couch. Her apartment wasn't tiny, it was cozy, she thought in defense as her gaze swept over the space. A small living room, an efficiency kitchen, one bedroom and a bathroom that, she had to admit, was so small she regularly smacked her elbows against the shower door. But the apartment walls were a soft, cheerful green and were dotted by framed photos of the beach, the mountains and her family.

"There," Gina said when she was back. "I took the baby to Jimmy. I have to pace when I'm mad."

Rita laughed. "Gina, I'm okay, really. I just needed to talk to you."

"Of course you did, but we're Italian and I need my hands to talk as much as I need to move around. Besides, I just finished feeding Kira. Jimmy can take her for a while."

Her sister had four gorgeous kids, the youngest only eight months old and a husband who adored her. A small pang of envy echoed in Rita's heart. Then to ease the hurt, she rubbed the mound of her baby with slow, loving strokes, and reminded herself that she had a child, too. That she wasn't alone. That it didn't matter that Jack had walked away from her only to suddenly crash back into her life.

"So," Gina said a moment later, "what're you going to do about this? How are you feeling?"

"I'm not sure, to both questions." Pushing up off the couch, Rita walked to the window overlooking Main Street and smiled, thinking Gina was right. Italians thought better when they could move around. Looking down on the street, she enjoyed the view that was so similar to the one she grew up with. Historic 25th Street in Ogden also had the old-fashioned, old-world feel to the buildings, the lampposts and the bright, jewel-toned flowers spilling out of baskets.

But as pretty as it was, it wasn't home. Not really. She was alone in the dark but for a slender thread of connection to her big sister.

"I don't know what to do," she admitted, "because I don't know what he's planning."

"Whatever it is, you can handle it." And, as if Gina had read her mind, she added, "You're not alone, Rita."

Her mouth curved slightly. "Not how it feels."

"You still love him, don't you?"

Rita laid her hand on the glass, letting the cold seep into her skin, chilling the rush of heat Gina's question had awakened.

"Why would I be foolish enough for that?" she whispered.

Three

"What's going on with you?"

Jack looked up. His father walked into the office that, up until four months ago, had been his. Thomas Buchanan was a tall man, with salt-and-pepper hair, sharp blue eyes and a still-trim physique. Though he'd abdicated the day-to-day running of the company to his oldest son, Thomas maintained his seat on the board and liked to keep abreast of whatever was happening. That included keeping tabs on his son.

"Nothing," Jack answered, lowering his gaze to the sheaf of papers on the desktop. "Why?"

"Well," Thomas said, strolling around the room, "you nearly bit Sean's head off when he couldn't get the shipping schedule up on the plasma fast enough."

"It's his job," Jack said, being perfectly reasonable. "He should be able to accomplish it when asked."

"Uh-huh."

Jack knew that tone. He glanced at his father, saw the wary curiosity-filled expression and looked away again. He wasn't in the mood for a chat and couldn't satisfy his father's curiosity. He knew that ever since he'd returned to civilian life, his family had been worried about him and no one more than his father. There didn't seem to be anything Jack could do about it, though. He didn't need therapy or sympathy and didn't want to talk about what he'd seen—what he wanted to do was forget about it and pick up his life where he'd left off. So far of course, that wasn't happening.

Rather than try to explain all of that to his dad, Jack chose to ignore the man's questions, even though he knew it wouldn't get him anywhere.

The worry would remain, along with the questions, whether spoken or not. After a few seconds of silence from him, though, Thomas seemed to understand that it was a subject Jack wasn't going to address.

"Still don't understand why you changed the office furniture around," his father said, surprising Jack with the sudden shift of topic. "My father's the one who put that desk in front of the windows. I don't think it's been moved since then. Until now."

Jack squirmed slightly in his oversize black leather chair. He'd made a few changes since he'd stepped into his father's shoes. The main one being that he had moved the old mahogany desk across the room so that he could have his back to a wall and not be outlined in a window.

Yes, he knew it was foolish without anyone pointing it out to him. He didn't have to worry about snipers here, but it was hard to shake ingrained habits that had kept him alive.

"I like it where it is," Jack said simply.

"Yeah." His father gave a resigned sigh, then admitted, "I wish you could talk to me."

His father's voice was so quiet, so wistful, Jack's attention was caught. He looked up and found his dad watching him through concerned eyes.

He didn't enjoy knowing that his family was worried about him. In fact, it only added to the guilt and the pain that were crouched on his shoulders every day. But he couldn't ease for them what he couldn't ease for himself.

"We do talk," Jack said.

"Not about anything important," his father answered. "Not since you got back. It's like you're still too far away to reach."

"I'm right here, Dad," he said, trying to help, knowing he was failing.

"Part of you is," his father agreed, "but not all of you. I wonder every day when my son will finally come home."

So did Jack. It was as if a piece of him had been left behind in the heat of a desert and he didn't know when or if he'd find that part of himself again. Jack sat back and let a long breath slide slowly from his lungs. "I'm doing my best here, Dad."

"I know that." Thomas stuffed his hands into his pants pockets and rocked uneasily on his heels. "I just wish there was something I could do to help. That you would *let* me do. I thought that stepping down, having you take over here, would make a difference. Drop you back into the world and, all right, *force* you to find your life again. But you continue to shut yourself off. From me, from your sister and brother. Hell, you haven't even been on a date since you got back, son."

"I don't want to date." Lie. Everything in him wanted Rita, but he wouldn't give in to it. He was in no shape to be in her life and he knew it.

"Right there should tell you that there's something wrong."

"I'm fine," Jack said, hoping to head his dad off at the pass. He'd heard this before. Knew that his father had the best of intentions. But Jack couldn't give the older man what he wanted most.

Thomas shook his head, then nodded. "You're

not, but you will be. I wish you could believe me on that." He walked toward his son, laid both hands on the desk and leaned in. "I know you don't. Not yet. But someday you will, Jack. Just give yourself a chance, all right?"

"I am." He looked into his father's eyes and lied again. "Everything's good. I swear."

Nodding, the older man pushed up from the desk. "Okay. We'll leave it there for now."

Thank God, Jack thought in relief.

"On another subject entirely," his father said, "I'm headed down to San Diego tomorrow. Sam and I are taking the boat out fishing for the weekend. Want to join us?"

The Buchanan Boys, as his mother used to call the three of them, had gone on hundreds of fishing weekends together. And in the old days, there had been nothing Jack liked more than getting away with his younger brother and his father. But now, the thought of being caged on a boat in the middle of the ocean with a too-curious father and brother sounded like a nightmare. They'd hammer him with questions, he'd resent being prodded and they'd all have a crappy time.

Besides, he told himself, there was Rita. Decisions to be made.

"I can't," he said. "I've got plans I can't get out of." Not that Rita knew of his plan to corner her into talking with him about their baby.

"Plans?" Thomas gave him a pleased smile. "That's good, son. Really good. To prove how happy that makes me, I won't even ask you what you're going to be doing."

"Thanks," Jack said wryly.

"All right, then." His father slapped his hands together then gave his palms a good scrub. "I've got to go by the house, pick up my fishing gear. Then I'm headed to San Diego. I'll have my phone with me if you need to contact me."

"I won't," Jack assured him. "But thanks. And say hi to Sam."

"I will."

Once his father was gone, Jack took a long, deep breath and willed the tension out of his body. It didn't work, so he got up, walked across the well-appointed office without even noticing the familiar furnishings.

Beige walls, dark red carpet, thick and plush enough to take a nap on, and twin couches facing each other across a low wood table. Windows were on two walls and Jack had moved the desk out of the line of sight of both of them.

Now, though, he walked to a far window and looked out over the sea. He didn't look at the beach below or the crowd of early-summer sun worshippers spread out on the sand. Instead, he watched the steady rise and fall of the water as wind and its own weight formed ripples and waves that seemed to go on endlessly.

It was quiet in the office and normally he treasured that. But now, that silence tapped at the edges of his mind like a persistent knock on a closed door. As that door opened, images of Rita flooded his brain, from before, from yesterday, until he half expected her to simply appear physically in the office. But that wasn't going to happen.

Rita would never come to him, she was too

angry and he couldn't blame her for it. But that wouldn't stop him from doing what he had to do. She was pregnant with *his* child and damned if he'd ignore that.

There was a knock on the office door just before it opened and his assistant stepped inside. A middle-aged woman with a brisk, no nonsense attitude, Linda Holloway said, "Excuse me, Mr. Buchanan, you've got a twelve-thirty meeting with the captain of *The Sea Queen*."

In the last four months, Linda had been responsible for Jack's seamless takeover of his father's position. She kept meticulous track of his schedule, his tasks and anything involving Buchanans. He was grateful, but right now, he didn't appreciate the interruption.

"The captain will meet you at the dock so you can take a walk-through of the areas you didn't see on your visit last month."

"Yeah," he said. "I remember." *The Sea Queen* was their latest ocean liner. And yes, he did have to meet the captain if only to go over any last-minute concerns about the ship's maiden voyage coming up in about a month. But not today.

"Cancel it," he snapped and stalked across the office.

"What?" Linda watched him, eyes wide. "But the captain has come in from his home in Arizona specifically for this meeting."

Yet one more guilt straw landed on the bale already situated on his shoulders, but he accepted it and moved on.

"It can't be helped. I've got personal business to take care of. Put the captain up in the best hotel in the city and tell him we'll meet tomorrow morning."

"But—"

"Eight o'clock on the dock. I'll be there and we can take care of this business then."

He snatched his suit jacket out of the closet and shrugged into it. What good was being the boss if you couldn't make the rules?

"But—"

"Linda," he said firmly, "I have somewhere to be and it can't wait. Make this happen."

"Yes, sir," she said, the slightest touch of defeat in her tone.

He didn't address it. "Thanks," he said and walked around her to leave without a backward glance.

"Tall, dark and dangerous is back."

Rita glanced at her friend and bakery manager, Casey. "What?"

She jerked her head toward the small cluster of tables in one corner of the bakery. "The guy who swept you out of here yesterday? He's back and looking just as edible as ever."

Rita's pulse skittered as she slowly, carefully, looked over her shoulder. Jack was sitting at the same table he'd spent hours at the day before. He wore a black suit, with a black dress shirt and a dark red tie. He looked exactly how Casey had described him. Dangerous. Edible.

As if he sensed her looking at him, he turned his head and his gaze locked with hers. Instantly, her blood turned to a river of fire and the pit of her stomach fluttered with nerves and expectation. He'd had that same effect on her from the beginning.

The minute he took her hand that first night on the beach, she'd felt it. That something special. Magical. There was a buzz between them that was electrifying.

She hadn't been afraid when he'd walked toward her out of the darkness. Maybe she should have been, but instead, it had felt almost as if she'd been waiting for him.

They walked to a small café, took a table on the sidewalk and ordered coffee. There they sat for three hours, talking, sharing their lives, though Rita did more of that than he did. He hadn't talked about his family or where he lived, only that his name was Jack Buchanan and that he had a week to be back in the real world and how he didn't want to waste a moment of it.

And when he walked her to her nearby hotel, neither of them wanted to say goodnight. He escorted her through the lobby to the bank of elevators with mirrored doors and she looked at their reflection as they stood together. He was so tall, she so short. But they seemed to fit, she thought, as if they'd been made for each other.

He turned her in his arms and asked, "Tomorrow? Be with me tomorrow, Rita."

"Yes," she said quickly, breathlessly.

"Good, that's good." A brief smile flashed across his face and warmed his cool blue eyes. "I'll be here early. Nine okay?"

"How about eight?" Rita asked, wanting to be with him again as soon as possible.

"Even better." He cupped her face in his palm and held her there as he bent his head to kiss her.

Rita held her breath and closed her eyes. Once, twice, his mouth brushed hers, gently, as if waiting for her response to know if there should be more.

And she wanted more. She wanted it all. Never had she felt for a man what Jack made her feel. Just talking with him stirred everything inside her and now that she knew the taste of his mouth, she hungered for him.

Rita answered his unasked question by wrapping her arms around his neck and leaning in to him. Her breasts pressed against his chest and her nipples ached as her body hummed. He actually growled and that sound sent her head spinning as he grabbed hold of her and deepened the kiss. Devouring her, his tongue tangled with hers, his breath mingled with hers and Rita felt as if their souls were touching, merging. Every inch of her body lit up and awakened as if she'd been in a coma all of her life and was only now truly living.

Neither of them cared about who might be watching, they were too lost in the fire enveloping them. Light-headed, loving the feel of his big strong hands sliding up and down her back, Rita could only think how badly she wanted him, but she wasn't a one-night stand kind of woman and didn't think she could pretend she was, even for Jack.

When finally she thought she might never breathe again, he broke the kiss and leaned his forehead against hers while they both fought to steady themselves.

"You are a dangerous woman," he whispered, a half smile curving his mouth.

"I never thought so, but okay."

His grin flashed. "Trust me."

She smiled back at him and felt her equilibrium disintegrate even further. Honestly, he didn't smile often, but when he did, it was a lethal weapon on a woman's defenses. Her mouth was still tingling from his kiss and the taste of him was flooding her system.

"Looking into those brown eyes of yours makes me feel like I'm diving into good, aged whiskey," he murmured, reaching out to smooth his fingers over her face. "Makes me a little drunk just losing myself in them."

"Your eyes remind me of the color of the sky after a mountain storm," she said, "clear, bright, with just a hint of shadow."

His smile faded then and Rita wished she could pull her words back. She hadn't meant to say anything about the darkness she saw in his eyes, but her urge to ease those shadows was nearly overwhelming.

"I've shadows enough, I guess," he admitted, letting his hand drop to his side. "But when I'm with you, I don't notice them."

"I'm glad," she said and went up on her toes to kiss him again.

Putting both hands on her shoulders, he held her in place and took a long step back. He shook his head and said, "If I kiss you again, I'm not going to be able to let you go."

That sounded pretty good to Rita, but she knew it wasn't smart to go to bed with a man she just met no matter how much she wanted to.

"So," he continued, "I'm going to leave while I still can."

"Probably a good idea," Rita said though, inside, her mind was whimpering, demanding that she beg him to stay.

"You keep looking at me with those whiskey eyes and I'm not going to be able to walk away." His voice was wry, his eyes flashing with heat.

"Then I will," she said, reaching out to punch the elevator call button.

"I do like a strong woman," he told her.

"Not so strong at the moment," Rita admitted when she looked at him again and felt a rush of heat settle and pool at her core. "But I will be. So, good night. I guess I'll see you at eight."

"Seven," he said.

"Even better," she said, throwing his own words from earlier back at him. The elevator dinged and the doors swished open. She stepped inside, then turned to look at him again. "Seven. I'll be ready."

"Good," he said as the doors slid shut on a whisper of sound, "because I'm ready now."

Alone, Rita leaned against the wall of the car, smiled to herself and lifted one hand to her mouth as if she could capture his taste and hold on to it forever. As the elevator rose to her floor, she told herself she wouldn't be getting much sleep tonight, but her morning was going to be wonderful.

"Rita?" Casey's voice and an insistent shake of her arm. "Hey, Rita? You okay?"

"What?" she tore her gaze from Jack's and looked at her friend. Coming up out of that memory that had been so filled with sensation and sound was like breaking the surface of the water when you were near drowning. You were back in reality but still too stunned to accept it easily. "Sure," she said, nodding for emphasis. "Yes. I'm fine. Really. Just…tired."

And sexually frustrated and angry and hurt and confused and far too many other emotions to even name.

"You sure?" Casey tried to steer Rita toward a stool. "Maybe you should sit down."

"No." Rita shook off all those unwelcome emotions and smiled. "I'm fine. Really. Um, will you keep an eye on the front while I go in the back to restock the cannoli tray?"

"Absolutely," Casey said, "as long as you call out if you need me."

"Don't be such a worrier," Rita told her with a pat on the arm.

Hurrying through the swinging door into the kitchen where she could get a couple of minutes to herself, Rita gave a sigh of relief to be on her own. She needed a little time to settle. Do the *ahooom* thing until she could breathe without feeling like she was going to shake apart at the seams.

"Get a grip, Rita," she mumbled as she snatched an apron off the hook by the door. Slipping it on over her head, she drew the string ties around her ever-expanding belly then tied it down. The simple, familiar task helped her get steady again.

She scrubbed her hands in the kitchen sink, dried them on a fresh towel, then turned to survey her domain. She might have chefs come in to help her, but this bakery was all hers, right down to the last cookie.

She was most comfortable in the kitchen. Rita and her brothers and sister had grown up working in their parents' Italian bakery in Ogden. From the time she was a little girl, barely tall enough to reach the mixing table, Rita had been helping the bakers. Even if it was just sprinkling flour on the cool white marble so dough could be rolled out. She loved the scent of baking cookies, cakes, pastries. She loved the feel of getting her hands into a huge bowl of dough to knead it. She'd worked off a lot of temper by working bread dough into shape.

"But there's not enough dough in the world to help me through *this*," she whispered, laying out paper doilies on a stainless steel tray. Then she moved to the end of the counter and carefully set fresh cannoli, some draped in shiny chocolate, on each doily. To her, presentation was as important as taste so before it went out to the shop, it would be perfect.

Once she was satisfied that all of her cannoli were lined up like soldiers, Rita checked on two more bowls of rising dough, punched them down, then covered them again, so they could do a second rise.

She'd be making bread before the bakery closed because her customers liked picking up a fresh loaf on the way home from work. Then she checked the meticulously aligned steel racks against one wall and made a note to have Casey get someone back there to box up the maple-nut biscotti.

"And I'm stalling," she said aloud to the empty room.

"Question is, why?"

Her eyes closed on a sigh as Jack's deep voice echoed all around her. Of course he wouldn't be ignored. He was the kind of man who got exactly what he wanted *when* he wanted it. A trait that was both sexy and annoying.

"You shouldn't be back here, Jack."

"Your friend Casey said you weren't feeling well."

She rolled her eyes and told herself to have a little chat with Casey. Wouldn't do any good, of course. If a gorgeous man asked Casey to stand on her head, the girl would. And they just didn't come more gorgeous than Jack, so Casey really had been putty in his hands.

Rita surrendered to the inevitable and turned around to face him. "I don't have time for you right now, Jack. I'm working."

She walked to the tray of fresh cannoli, but before she could pick it up, Jack swooped in and snatched it from her. "You shouldn't be carrying this. It's heavy."

A thread of pleasure whipped through her at his instinctive urge to protect, even as it irritated her that he clearly thought she was either helpless or a delicate blossom.

"I carry heavy things all the time. I'm pregnant, not an invalid." He opened his mouth to argue the point, but she rushed on before he could. "I'm careful, too. I don't take chances with my baby—"

"Our baby."

"*The* baby," she corrected meaningfully. "Now, give me the tray."

"Don't be stupid," he said and turned for the door into the front of the shop.

"I'm stupid now?" she said to his retreating back.

"I said *don't* be stupid. There's a difference."

When the door swung open, snatches of conversation rushed toward her, along with Casey's prolonged sigh of "Thank you so much."

Rolling her eyes so hard it was a wonder they didn't simply pop out of her skull and skitter across the floor, Rita pulled down the decorative biscotti boxes. She'd pack them herself and that would give her yet another reason to stay back here and keep her distance from Jack. Of course she should have known that wouldn't work.

He came back through the swinging door, holding an empty tray and shook his head at her. "Do you have to do everything around here personally?"

"My business, my responsibility." She lifted a tray of biscotti off the rack and turned for the counter, dodging Jack when he would have taken it from her. "So yes, I do. I want things done a certain way and I can't expect everyone else to do all the work."

She expertly folded the box into shape, slid a dozen biscotti inside then closed the box and slapped a gold *Italia* sticker in place. Automatically, she started on the next one while Jack came closer. Rita didn't even look up from her task when she asked, "Why are you here again, Jack?"

He picked up a biscotti and took a bite, shrugging when she gave him a hard look. "I'm here because you are. Because my baby is. And I'm not leaving until we work this out between us."

"Fine." She continued boxing the biscotti in the

bright red *Italia* containers, keeping her eyes on the job, rather than him. If she looked at Jack again she'd feel that torn sensation—yearning and betrayal.

He'd allowed her to mourn. Let her believe he was dead. How did you forgive someone for that when they wouldn't even explain *why* they'd done it? And how did you get past those old feelings that continually slipped in despite the pain that should have smothered them?

"You want to talk, let's talk," she said. "I'll start. I want to know why you disappeared."

"That's not on the table."

Now she did risk a quick glance at him and his features were tight, closed, his eyes cold and icy.

"So we talk, but only about what you're willing to discuss?" Shaking her head, she sealed another box and set it aside, automatically reaching for the next.

"I'm not looking to recapture anything here, Rita."

A sharp stab of pain stole her breath at the blunt honesty. She looked into his eyes. "Wow."

He flinched slightly, but otherwise remained stoic. "I'm not saying that to hurt you."

"And yet…"

He looked down at the biscotti in his hand and then lifted his gaze to hers again. "This isn't about us, Rita. It's about the baby."

A sinking sensation opened up in the pit of her stomach. Her mouth went dry and her hands shook, so she set the box she was holding down onto the counter so he couldn't see it. How had they come to this, she wondered. Where had it all gone so terribly wrong?

What had made him shut her out when he left her to go back to his duties? What had turned him away from what they'd found, what they'd been to each other for one amazing week?

And how had he become so cold that he could stand just inches from her and look at her as if she wasn't really there?

"What is it you want, Jack?"

He set the biscotti down, planted both palms on the counter and said, "I want you to marry me."

Four

Rita actually *felt* shock slam into her like a physical blow. Whatever she'd been expecting hadn't been this. She knew she was staring. Knew she should say *something*, but for the first time in her life she was absolutely speechless. He was serious, that much she could see. But surely he didn't expect her to agree.

He laughed shortly, but it was merely a harsh scrape of sound against his throat. There was no humor in his eyes and no easing of the tightness of his mouth. "Not the usual reaction when a man proposes."

Finally she found her own voice. "It's not the *usual* situation, is it?"

"No," he admitted solemnly, "it's not."

"Jack, you don't want to be married to me." God, how it hurt to say that, because six months ago, at the end of their week together, Rita had had dreams. She'd believed that when he came home from war, they would get married, have kids, live happily ever after. All the normal fantasies that women spin when they meet a man who makes their blood burn and their heart sing.

But that dream had died with him, or so she'd believed at the time. Now he was here, but it was a different Jack who faced her asking her to marry him. It was a colder, harder man than she'd once known and the loss of that rang deep and true inside her.

He pushed one hand through his hair then scrubbed the back of his neck. "No," he admitted, looking directly into her eyes. "I don't want to be married. To anyone."

"Then what is this about?"

"I also don't want my kid born without my name."

Rita sighed heavily. "Of course you'll be on the birth certificate, listed as the father."

He frowned. "Not what I'm talking about. I want us married when the baby's born," he told her firmly. "After that, we can divorce and I won't bother you again."

Just when she thought the shocks couldn't be more earth shattering, he said something else that ripped away what was left of the earth beneath her feet. "Seriously?"

Moments ago, she'd worried about a custody battle, but in reality he wanted nothing to do with his own child? What kind of man was he?

He blew out a breath, shoved his hands into his slacks pockets and admitted, "I'm not asking you to understand—"

"Good," she interrupted. "Because I don't. If you don't want me, then fine. I get it. But how can you not want anything to do with your own child? My God, who are you?"

"Still me," he insisted, but she didn't believe him.

When she first met him, he'd been more quiet

than chatty, more solemn than happy, but there hadn't been such a marked coldness about him. Now it was as if he'd submerged his old self under a layer of ice.

"Think whatever you like about me. Can't change it. But I want my kid born into the Buchanan family." His mouth tightened and the muscle in his jaw twitched as if he were grinding his teeth together. "After that, you can raise it."

It. So impersonal. So distancing. Rita hadn't wanted to know what her baby was, preferring to be surprised. But now, at her next appointment, she would ask. Because she wanted Jack to see their child as a *person.* But that was for later. "So you'll just put your baby aside like you did me and move on, is that it?"

He scrubbed one hand across his jaw. "You're putting words in my mouth."

"Because you're not explaining any of this."

"Damn it, Rita, you don't have to make this harder than it already is."

"No, I don't," she said sadly. "Because *you* did that just fine on your own."

"I'll make sure you're taken care of."

Her eyes nearly popped out of her head at that insult on top of everything else. Rita had reached her limit. She walked around the edge of the counter, leading with her belly, and didn't stop until she was standing in front of him. "You think I want *money* from you?"

He met her gaze and Rita would have given anything to be able to read what he was thinking, feeling. But there was no clue there for her. He was a blank slate. Deliberately. This new Jack had such a tight handle on his emotions, she couldn't see past the facade.

"No," he said, shaking his head. "I know you don't want money."

"That's something, anyway," she muttered, still looking up into his eyes, still looking for some shred of the man she'd loved.

"Do this, Rita," he said quietly.

"Why would I marry you knowing you don't want me?"

"Because I need it," he admitted and it looked as though it cost him to give her that much. "I need to know my kid has my name. That I did the right thing."

"The right thing." She huffed out a breath and folded her arms across her growing middle. "This isn't the '50s, Jack. Single mothers do just fine on their own and so can I." She didn't believe in what he was saying, but Jack clearly did.

Rita knew she would be fine raising her child alone. She had her family's support. She had her own business, a home and the strength to do whatever she had to do to succeed.

"It's not a matter of that," Jack argued. He picked up the biscotti again and when his hand fisted around it, let crumbs fall to the marble counter. "I know you *could* do it. I don't want you to. I get you don't owe me a damn thing and I've got no right to ask for this. Still, this is important to me, Rita. I don't want my kid knowing his parents weren't married."

"Oh, for heaven's—"

"Look, this is the best answer for all of us," Jack said quickly.

"How is a meaningless marriage the best for anyone? You're crazy."

"That's been said before," he admitted wryly. "But not about this. This is important enough to me that I'm not going to back off or give up until you agree."

She laughed shortly, turned her back on him and went back to boxing biscotti. "Good luck with that."

"I'm a rich man, Rita," he said and brought her up short.

Money again? What was he getting at? A tiny nugget of fear settled in the pit of her belly as, wary now, she asked, "How rich?"

"Very."

She took a breath. He was watching her, waiting for her reaction and she wasn't sure what that should be. Rita didn't care if he had all the money in the world or nothing at all. So what was the point of this?

"Congratulations to you," she finally said. "But why should I care?" Even as she asked that question, though, her brain was racing. A *very* rich man? She'd had no idea.

But then, there was so much she didn't know about him. He hadn't talked about himself a lot during their week together and she'd told herself that the information would come. That they could learn about each other in letters, phone calls. But that had never happened, so she was as much in the dark now as she had been then.

A very rich man, though, had power. The question was now, would he use that power to manipulate her, to take custody of her child?

"I can take care of the baby," he said.

She stiffened. "So can I."

"Rita, you live above a bakery," he snapped. "I can get you a nice place. On the beach."

"Are you trying to bribe me?" she asked, astounded at the turn this conversation was taking.

"No. Look, it's my kid, too." He took a moment to gather his thoughts and said, "We get married, I get you a house and after the baby's born, we split up."

"And if I don't want to marry you?"

"You will."

"Don't take any bets on it."

"I will bet on it." He held out one hand. "Five bucks."

"For a *very* rich man, you don't have much faith in your ability to persuade me." She shook his hand and deliberately ignored the zip of heat she felt. "Twenty dollars."

"Even better," he said and completely knocked her feet out from under her.

Even better. It reminded her of that first night, of his smile, his kiss, their eagerness to be together. And when she looked into his eyes, she saw a gleam of amusement and knew he was remembering, too. Her heart turned over at the tiny glimpse of *her* Jack. Maybe he wasn't as lost as she'd thought. Maybe he was reachable.

He let go of her hand but the heat engendered remained. The tiny moment of shared memory was over, the hint of humor gone from his eyes and she was left with this gorgeous stranger again. How could he make her feel so much while apparently feeling nothing himself? How could she allow herself to marry a man for all the wrong reasons when she once would have given anything to marry him for *love*?

"It won't work, Jack."

"We'll see, Rita."

It took her only a week to surrender.

A week of Jack coming to the bakery daily, helping out, making sure she got off her feet. He ignored his own business and showed up in jeans, scuffed cowboy boots and T-shirts, making her heart skip just looking at him. He stacked pallets of supplies, carried trays of cookies, rang up sales and won Casey over. That last part wasn't hard at all, Rita allowed. But as for the rest, he wore her down with his relentless pursuit and dogged determination.

"You owe me twenty bucks," he said when she told him she'd marry him.

"This isn't funny." Should she have held out? Refused him? Possibly. But in the last week, she'd caught repeated glimpses of the old Jack, and though they were brief, they'd given her enough hope to think that just maybe it was worth trying to get past the ice he'd packed around his heart.

"No one's laughing."

"I'll marry you, but I can't get married without my family there," she said. "They'd never understand."

They weren't going to understand a quickie wedding or a divorce so soon after that wedding, either, but one problem at a time.

"Fine. Us. Our families. Small ceremony," Jack said like he was ticking things off a to-do list.

"And I don't want anyone to know this is a... business deal," she said for lack of a better way to put it. "Also, I don't want you to buy me a house."

"Nonnegotiable," he said. "When we split, you can pick something out or I will."

It didn't make sense to argue with him now, but Rita could be as stubborn as Jack. And she wouldn't be bought off or given a "going away gift." But this, too, was a worry for another day. God knew she had enough for today already.

"Okay, then," she said, sighing heavily. "I guess we're getting married."

He grabbed a black leather jacket off a hook by the back door and shrugged into it. "I'll take care of the details. I'll send packers to get your stuff out of your apartment. Bring it to the penthouse."

She blinked at him. "Packers?"

He stopped, looked at her. "You want this to look real, then we'll be living together at my place."

At his place? She didn't even know *where* he lived! Oh, this wasn't something she'd even thought about.

Before she could say anything to that, though, he was gone.

"It's a surprise, that's all I'm saying," Jack's sister, Cass, said for the tenth time in the last hour. "I'm glad you found someone, but it would have been nice to meet her before the wedding."

He looked at Cass and read the worry in her eyes. God, would he ever get used to seeing that emotion on his family's faces? And if not accustomed to it, could he please, God, reach a point where it wouldn't tear at him? "It was sudden. I met her six months ago—"

"Clearly," Cass said wryly.

"Right." The baby. His family had been shocked not only with the announcement that he was getting married, but that he was going to be a father. Soon.

Cass flipped her long brown hair behind her shoulder, threaded her arm through his and watched Rita with her family. "I like her already."

"Good. That's good." Jack nodded thoughtfully and kept his gaze locked on his wife. *Wife.* He swallowed hard and told himself it would be all right. The important thing here was that he'd done the right thing by his kid. He could survive three months of marriage and then his life would go back to what it had been. Quiet. Alone.

"Jack?"

He looked at his sister and nearly sighed. She was watching him so closely, trying to read every expression on his face, he might as well have been under a microscope. But judging by her own expression, she wasn't happy with what she was seeing. In fact, she was giving him the serious, concerned look he was pretty sure she gave her patients.

As a general practitioner, Cass was adept at cutting through the bull to make a diagnosis and it was clear to him she didn't like what she was seeing in him.

"Relax, Cass," he said, "I'm fine."

"Sure. It's what you've been saying for months."

"Then you should believe me," he said, patting her hand on his arm.

"No, you remind me of this one patient. He's ten. And he always insists he's fine even when his fever is spiking or his throat is sore." She shook her head. "He doesn't want me asking questions, you see. And neither do you."

"Yeah," Jack said, giving her a tired smile. "But I'm not one of your patients."

"Good thing," she told him. "We'd butt heads even more than we do now. Jack, I have to ask you something. Will you let her in?"

"What?" He looked down at her and tried to hide his impatience. It wasn't the family's fault that he couldn't give them what they wanted. *Be* who they wanted.

Cass moved to stand in front of him and put both of her hands on his forearms. "I'm asking you. You're married now. Going to be a father. And yet I still see that distance in your eyes."

He let his head fall back and he stared unseeing at the overcast gray sky for a second or two. The steady roar of the ocean was a constant white noise in the background. The sea itself was as gray as the sky and the waves rolling to shore just a few feet away were edged with foam that looked like lace.

"Cass..."

"Don't bother to deny it. We all know it's true. You've shut down, Jack and we don't know how to reach you." She leaned in and looked up into his eyes. "Will you let Rita try?"

What no one understood was, he couldn't allow himself to be reached. Couldn't be pulled from the shadows because the darkness was where he belonged now. He felt his own helplessness rise as he watched his sister's face.

Jack wished he could reassure his whole family. Wished that this marriage was changing something. But the truth was, *nothing* had changed for him. He was who he was now and everyone would eventually accept what he already had.

The old Jack Buchanan died on his last tour.

Cass must have read the resignation on his features because she sighed, went up on her toes to kiss his cheek. "I love you, Jack. Give yourself a chance to be happy."

He nodded again, gave her a quick hug, and then sighed in relief when she walked off to join her family. Jack looked to his father and brother as they stood with Rita's parents, laughing and talking. There was no respite for Jack today. He'd dropped himself into a crowd. Yet he was still a man on the sidelines, watching as life went on around him.

Both families were gathered and they seemed to be getting along fine. His sister's family, husband and two kids and his brother Sam's group, wife and three kids, actually looked small compared to Rita's.

Her parents, her sister and two brothers with all of their kids and spouses made quite a crowd. Her sister's four kids, each brother had five and one of the wives was as pregnant as Rita. The Marchettis were clearly devoted to family and Jack was glad to see it. When this marriage ended, when he was out of her life, Rita would have their support to help her through.

Another straw of guilt dropped onto his shoulders and he nearly winced at the added weight. Had he done the right thing here? Marrying her with the promise to divorce in three months? Setting her up to have to explain what went wrong to a loving family who were assuming she was marrying for love? Wouldn't it have been better to just tell everyone the truth up front?

Easier for him, maybe, he acknowledged. But for Rita? His gaze went to her and locked on with a laser focus. Tension gripped him as every cell in his body tightened, buzzing with the kind of need only *she* had ever awakened in him. He wanted her with every breath and knew he couldn't have her because he had nothing to offer her. Not now.

All he could give her was this marriage and a house and the promise to stay the hell out of her way once this was done and over. She deserved at least the pretense of a real marriage for her family's sake, he told himself. Hell, she deserved so much more than he had.

Her curly brown hair was pulled up on top of her head to cascade down past her shoulders in a riot of wind-tossed curls. She wore a long dress of some filmy material that almost seemed otherworldly. The color was a soft lavender so pale it made him think of moonlit fog. Her eyes were bright, her mouth curved in a smile as she hugged her sister. Then those aged, whiskey eyes found his and his insides fisted. He was caught in a trap of his own making.

Married to a woman he wanted and couldn't have. Living in a shadow world, yearning for light. Wanting to bury himself inside her warmth to ease the cold that was always crouched within him. He was outside a window staring in at what he most desired, but unable to reach out and touch it.

And maybe that was his penance, he thought. The price he had to pay for living.

"You look too solemn for a man on his wedding day."

Somehow Jack's father had sneaked up on him. Damn. He'd been hyperalert for months, but looking at Rita was enough to distract him from everything but her.

"Just thinking," he said.

Thomas turned to follow Jack's gaze to Rita. "Well, I don't know how you can look at your bride and be thinking thoughts dark enough to put a scowl on your face."

Chagrined, Jack realized he hadn't been paying close enough attention. He'd let his mask slip and shown people what he was feeling and that wasn't something he wanted to happen. No point in those he loved worrying even more than they already were.

He forced a smile and hoped it looked more real than it felt. "You like her?"

Thomas smiled and slapped his back. "What's not to like? She's beautiful, kind and she's giving me another grandchild." His voice trailed off. "I only wish your mother was still here to enjoy all of these kids running around."

Jack smiled wistfully. His mother had died five years before and had only seen a few of the grandchildren she would have enjoyed so much. "She would have loved this."

"Yes, she would," his father said. "But I have a feeling she's here, somehow. I can't imagine your mother *not* being around when something big was happening to one of her kids."

True, Jack thought. And his mother never would have worried about him from afar. She would have hammered at him relentlessly until she'd dragged him kicking and screaming out of the darkness and back to where she wanted him. Carla Buchanan had been a force of nature. And Jack honestly didn't know if he was more sad or relieved that his mom wasn't there to see what he'd come to.

"Come on now," his father said. "We're all

going over to *The Queen Mary* for the wedding brunch."

He had to smile. Once his father had heard about the wedding, he'd insisted on taking care of a celebratory brunch. And of course, he'd arranged for a private dining room on *The Queen Mary*. Nothing his father liked better than ships, and in his defense, Jack was sure their out-of-town guests would enjoy visiting the historical ship.

"You go ahead," Jack said, "I'll be there in a minute."

"All right then."

Thomas walked off to join the others and Jack took a breath, steeling himself to join in, to be a part of the festivities. The stretch of beach had never looked longer to him. A cold sea wind whipped past him and tugged at the edges of his jacket. He headed for their families, but with every step he took, he felt the sand shifting beneath his feet and the sensation reminded him of too much.

Awakened too many memories that were always too close to the surface. His insides tightened and a heightened sense of awareness took over. Sounds were more defined, until he could hear shrieks from down the beach and screams that had him whirling around and crouching as if he were under fire. Then his gaze locked on a screaming girl as her boyfriend carried her into the icy water.

Heartbeat racing, hands fisting at his sides, Jack took a breath to steady himself. The wind pushed at him, but instead of scenting sea spray on the air, he smelled the stale, flat air of a desert country that had claimed too much of him. His spine stiffened, but he turned back and kept walking, determined to keep what he was feeling to himself.

To stay half in the shadows even as he pretended to be in the light.

Rita walked up to meet him and he looked into her eyes, focusing on her, only her. Staring at her, the swamping sensations nearly drowning him faded, to be replaced by a different kind of tension. She was so beautiful she stole his breath. And now she was his wife.

God help her.

Five

"I didn't let anything slip to Mom and Dad," Gina was saying. "*But*, I know there's more to this whole sudden wedding thing than you're telling."

Rita glanced past her sister to the people in the private dining room. Sure that no one could overhear, she said, "Okay, yes. There is more. Thanks for not saying anything, and I'll tell you about it at some point, I promise. Just… I can't right now and I don't want Mom and Dad worrying."

"I know how to keep a secret." Gina's eyes narrowed on her. "So I'll stay quiet. But I'm warning you, Rita, if he's a jerk, I expect you to tell me so I can kick him."

Rita laughed a little as relief trickled through her. She had enough on her mind and heart at the moment without worrying about her family worrying about *her*. Gina was always as good as her word. If she said she'd keep a secret, nothing and no one would be able to pry it out of her.

If her family knew she'd gotten married with the promise of a quickie divorce looming, there would no doubt be hell to pay. As it was, her brothers kept giving Jack a hard eye like they'd prefer to take him outside and deal with the man who'd left their sister pregnant and alone. But her parents at least were believing Rita's story of finding Jack and the two of them reigniting the love between them.

If only, Rita thought with an internal sigh.

"I promise. But, I might kick him myself before you get the chance."

"I can live with that," Gina said, sipping on a mimosa in a crystal champagne flute.

While her sister was quiet, Rita had a minute

to think about her wedding day. The ceremony had been small, just hers and Jack's families on a roped-off area of the beach. The early June weather of dark skies and cool winds had kept the beach mostly deserted, so it had been intimate in spite of being so public.

When they exchanged vows, Rita remembered looking deeply into Jack's eyes and for one brief moment, she'd seen that quick glimpse of *her* Jack hidden inside him again. And that gave her hope. Maybe there was a way to reach him. To *actually* reignite what they'd shared so briefly six months ago.

Their kiss at the end of the ceremony had started off perfunctory, but after a split second, it was as if Jack had forgotten that they were putting on a show. He'd pulled her in to him and cradled her against his body as his mouth took hers in a slow, seductive kiss that had nearly blown Rita's short veil right off her head.

If there was *that* between them still, that heat, that magic, couldn't there be more? Heat didn't exist in a vacuum. Emotions, feelings, had to be there, too, right?

Was she being deliberately foolish? Probably. But if you didn't try, you couldn't win. If you didn't ask, the answer was always no.

"You're thinking."

"That's a bad thing?" she asked, a small smile curving her mouth.

"I haven't decided yet," Gina admitted. She half turned to look at Jack, across the room, standing somewhat apart from everyone else. "He's gorgeous, I give you that. But he doesn't seem the sociable type. Won't that drive you nuts?"

Rita shook her head. "No, I talk enough for both of us."

"True." Gina laughed.

"You know, he wasn't like this when we first met," Rita said quietly. "Oh, he never talked as much as I do, but he was warmer. Less…closed down. I don't know how to explain it."

"You're doing pretty well," Gina said thoughtfully, studying the man they were talking about.

"Gina, the thing is, every once in a while," Rita

continued, "I see the real Jack hiding behind his eyes."

Her sister gave her a cool look. "And you think you can bring him out of hiding?"

"If not me, who?" Rita asked. "If there's a chance, I have to try."

Gina dropped one arm around her shoulders. "Sweetie, sometimes people are hiding for a reason."

She might be right, Rita acknowledged. But if she didn't find out for sure, the what-if would haunt her forever. "But what if that reason can be dealt with? Fought?"

"Oh, God," Gina murmured, shaking her head. "You're trying to save him, aren't you?"

Was she? Oh, Rita didn't like the sound of that. How many times had she seen friends fall for a guy with "issues" and then try to fix him? Get him to change. Help him deal with his demons? Is that what she was doing?

No, she argued with herself silently. This was different. *Jack* was different. Something specific had happened to him and whatever it was had affected him deeply. Even if it was because of what they'd once had, or the fact that they'd created a child together... Didn't Rita owe it to him to at least make the attempt to help him?

"Is that so wrong?" She looked at her sister, really curious to hear what she had to say.

"No, I guess not," Gina said, resignation clear in her tone. "If it's something you feel like you have to do, there's no stopping you anyway. Just make sure you don't lose yourself in the effort."

"I won't," Rita said and knew that keeping her promise wasn't going to be easy. Because in spite of everything that had happened between them, Jack was the one man in the world who could still cause her pain.

"Uh-oh," Gina said suddenly, "I've gotta go save Jimmy. Mom's just dropped Kira into his lap, so he's got all four kids and is seriously outnumbered."

Rita smiled on cue, but she wasn't thinking about her brother-in-law. Her thoughts were with Jack, standing apart and alone at his own wedding. Backlit by the light flooding in through the wall of windows he stood in front of, he looked so solitary, it broke her heart.

He'd done all he could to make this faux marriage beautiful for her. From the ceremony itself to this family reception. *The Queen Mary* was a beautiful old ship and this private dining room in its five-star restaurant was old-world elegant. Windows lined both sides of the ship and she imagined that when the old ocean liner was still sailing, the views were incredible.

Where Jack stood, there was a sweeping vista of the sea and other boats bobbing on the surface. The sun had finally broken through the clouds and slanted off the water like gold dust. But Jack was silhouetted, defining his aloneness, and that tore at Rita.

"We're staying in town for a few days," Gina was saying. "As long as we're here, figured we'd take the kids to Disneyland."

Rita glanced at her. "They'll love it."

"Yep," Gina mused. "Hope Jimmy and I survive it." She grabbed Rita's hand and squeezed. "If you need me for anything, call me. I'll be there."

"I know," she said, returning that squeeze briefly. "Thanks, Gina. I'm gonna be fine."

As Gina moved away, Rita heard her own words echo in her mind and she hoped she was right. Because at the moment, her heart was aching for the man who'd cut himself off. He'd gone to so much trouble for her, but he wasn't being a part of this at all. Even in the heart of his family, he was determinedly alone. That didn't equate with everything he'd told her about his family when they met. Back then, he'd laughed at the stories of fishing trips with his father and brother, of his sister being outwitted by her five-year-old daughter, of how devastated their family had been when they'd lost Jack's mother.

Now, though, it was as if his family wasn't even in the same room with him. She'd seen his father, brother and sister try to connect with him and eventually give up. She'd watched Jack keep to the sidelines as if punishing himself, somehow. Rita didn't have the first clue how to go about reaching him, but she knew she had to try. Because if there was even a tiny chance she could find *her* Jack, it would be worth the effort.

Smiling and nodding to her family as she passed, Rita walked to Jack. He was staring out at the ocean and Rita came up right beside him.

He didn't look at her, but he must have sensed her presence. "Everything all right?"

"It's fine," she said, staring up at his profile, waiting for some flicker of—she didn't even know what. "Are *you* okay?" she asked.

He turned his head then and looked down at her. She felt that stare sizzle in her blood. One look from him and she burned.

"Yeah," he said finally, quietly. "I'm just not good in a crowd of people."

His words, so simply stated, tugged at her heart as she realized just how important this marriage must have been to him. He'd dropped himself into a situation that would make him uncomfortable because this meant something to him. He'd stood up against what plagued him to make sure she had what she needed at the wedding. He'd brought her family in, and seen to it that everything was beautiful for her in spite of his own misgivings. Just another sign to Rita that her Jack was in there somewhere. That only strengthened her resolve to discover what had happened to change the man she'd once thought was her one and only.

But today, she only wanted to be here. With him. To let him know he wasn't alone, even if that's what he believed he wanted. Going on instinct, she slid her hand into his and was rewarded when his fingers curled around hers and held tight.

Jack lay wide awake in bed, alone on his wedding night.

Rita was down the hall in the penthouse guest-room and he couldn't tear his mind away from the image of her. His whole body ached for her, just as it had from the first moment he'd met her.

No other woman had ever affected him as she had. While he was overseas, he'd worked on convincing himself that what he'd felt with her was nothing special. He'd had to, just to survive. Clinging to the real world and the memories of a woman with a warm heart, soft body and wild, raw laugh had only made his reality that much harder to endure.

Then, when everything went to hell one afternoon, Jack had sliced every emotion out of his life because it was imperative to survival. He hadn't written to her because he couldn't lie to her about what was going on and he couldn't have told her the truth. He didn't look for her when he came back because he was in no shape to be around anyone. And because by then, he knew he could never again be the man she had once known.

"But Fate's a nasty bitch," he muttered into the darkness. His own voice seemed to echo, low and harsh in the empty room.

The gods of irony had conspired against him. He'd put so much effort into avoiding her that the gods laughed and threw her in his path, making it impossible to ignore her. And now they were married.

Shaking his head, he draped one arm across his eyes to dim the moonlight spearing into his bedroom. He had the terrace doors open, because he couldn't stand to be closed in. He needed that swirl of air, even when it was cold. Needed to smell the sea, remind himself that he was here. Home. And not in that hot, desperate situation that had nearly driven him over the edge.

His room was big, with a black-and-white-tiled gas hearth on one wall, bookcases and a television on the other walls. There were chairs, tables and a bed that was so big it felt even emptier than it actually was.

"My choice," he reminded himself and gritted his teeth against the roiling heat and tension coiled inside him.

It would be so easy to go down the hall, walk into her room and relive a few memories. Make some new ones. No guarantee she'd let him in, but then he remembered how she'd held his hand at the reception. As if she'd known, somehow sensed, that he'd needed that touch to ground himself in the moment.

She was good like that, he thought. Always had been. They'd connected so deeply in one week that it had been almost like they could read each other's minds. He hoped to hell she couldn't pick up on his thoughts now, but back then, it was different.

He was there the next morning to pick her up at seven, as agreed. She was in the lobby, waiting for him, clearly as eager as he was for them to be together again. Just seeing her in her jeans and dark green sweater had made his mouth water.

When she smiled at him, he went hard as stone and damn near killed himself just trying to walk across the floor toward her. Then she reached out for him, took his hand and he was lost in need, heat, a fire that built with every breath.

They had breakfast on the beach, coffee and bagels shared over laughter and a breathless sense of expectation. Looking into her whiskey-brown eyes was mesmerizing. Intoxicating. On that deserted winter beach, they were alone in the world but for one or two hardy surfers out challenging the waves.

Hands linked, they walked along the beach for what felt like miles, then they hiked back to the car and drove down the coast. Music pumping, wind roaring through the open windows and the two of them, still holding hands, as if unable to bear not touching.

Two hours later they were in San Diego and stopping for lunch at a tiny inn outside La Jolla. The once-dignified old Victorian mansion clung to the cliffside and waves pounded against the rocks in a steady, rhythmic heartbeat.

"It's beautiful here," Rita said, letting her gaze slide across the water, the cliffs and the meticulously tended gardens.

"Yeah, it is," he replied, his gaze locked on her. With the wind in her hair and the winter sun shining in her eyes, Jack thought he'd never seen anything more lovely. And he knew if he didn't kiss her soon, it would kill him.

"You're not even looking at the view," she chided with a half smile.

"Depends on what you consider a great view." He snaked one hand across the small round table and covered hers. He felt her pulse pounding in time with the relentless sea and knew that beat matched his own, too.

She licked her lips and he fought to breathe. She curled her hand beneath his and the heat that blossomed between them should have set the grounds on fire.

Her gaze locked with his. "What's happening here?" she asked, her voice nearly lost in the wind and the roar of the waves.

"Whatever it is, I'm all for it," he admitted and stroked his thumb across her palm. Her eyes glazed over and her breath quickened.

"Oh, I am, too."

"You're making me crazy, Rita. Couldn't sleep last night. I kept thinking about you. About today. About..."

She pulled in a shaky breath. "I've been thinking about...too."

Oh, yeah. If he didn't have her soon, he was a walking dead man. He'd never make that two- or three-hour drive home with his body and mind so entangled with nothing but thoughts of her. All he could think of was touching her, stroking her skin, sliding his body into hers and being surrounded by her heat.

"You know, maybe we should book a room here at the inn. Neither one of us slept much last night. We could get some sleep before that long drive back up to Orange County."

Her tongue slipped out again to slide across her bottom lip and his gaze tracked that motion as if his life depended on it. Fire, he thought. It felt like he was burning up from the inside and if his body got any harder, he'd have to crawl from the table because walking would be impossible.

Nodding, she said, "That's probably a good idea. A nap, I mean. Tired drivers can be dangerous."

"Yeah," he agreed. "Safety first."

Her smile was fleeting, but brilliant, taking his breath away. "I'll see if they've got a room where we can...rest. Just wait here."

When he stood up, Rita took his hand and squeezed. "Okay, I'll wait. But hurry. I'm really tired."

That was all the encouragement Jack needed.

In ten minutes, they were entering their room on the second floor. Jack swept her up close to him, kicked the door closed and gave the dead bolt a fast turn. She laughed up into his face and he felt something inside him turn over. She was more than he'd ever had. More than he'd ever thought to find. And for now, she was all his.

"Oh," she said, tearing her gaze from his to give the room a quick look. "Isn't it lovely?"

He hadn't noticed. Now he did. White lace curtains at the windows, a brass bed with a detailed flower quilt across the mattress. There were two chairs before a tiny hearth outlined in sea-blue tiles and a table held a carafe of water and two glasses. There was a door that led to a private bath and photographs of old San Diego dotted the pale gold walls.

He supposed it was very nice, though it could have been a cave for all he cared. "Yeah," he said tightly, not caring about the room.

When she looked up at him again, she gave him a knowing smile. "Ready to nap?"

"More than you know."

"Then let's get to sleep," she said, throwing her

arms around his neck, holding on as she lifted her face for his kiss.

When their mouths met, merged, it was like the whole damn world lit up. Or maybe it was just the fire inside, blazing brighter than ever. Seconds ticked into minutes and still they stood, locked together, bodies pressed tightly to each other, heartbeats hammering in time.

Finally, he tore his mouth free, fought for enough breath to admit, "I have to touch you."

"Please, yes," she said softly, hungrily, "Now. Touch me."

In seconds, they were naked and falling onto the bed together. Afternoon light poured through the windows and winter sun painted a soft, golden slash across the polished wood floor to lie on the bed and shine in Rita's eyes.

His gaze raked over her lush curves, and everything in him stirred to a fever pitch. Jack felt as though he'd been waiting for this one moment his whole life. He bent his head to take one of her nipples into his mouth. Tasting, nibbling, working his teeth and tongue across her sensitive skin.

Every whispered moan and sigh that slipped from her fed his hunger until it was like a closed fist around his throat, making breathing almost impossible. Her fingers slid through his military-short hair, nails scraping along his scalp as she arched up and into him, silently asking for more. And he had plans for a lot more.

Lifting his head, he stared down into her eyes. "This could be the longest nap on record."

"Oh, good," she said on a long sigh, "because I'm really tired."

He grinned. "And I'm really glad to hear that."

She pulled his head down to hers and this time she claimed his mouth in a kiss that seared him right to his bones. He let her lead, let her devour and gave back all that she was giving him and still, it wasn't enough.

Jack moved over her, running his hands up and down her body, discovering every curve, exploring her soft silky skin until they were both trembling with an explosive need. Her small hands moved over his chest, his shoulders and every stroke of her fingers felt like licks of flame.

They rolled across the bed, tasting, touching. Her heavy brown curls spread out beneath her head like a wild, tangled dark halo. He was lost in her, her scent, her touch, the hunger raging inside him. Body raging, mind fogging over, Jack stood poised on the brink of a cliff.

"Now," she whispered, lifting her hips, rocking into his hand as he cupped her center. "Jack, now. I can't take this anymore."

"Hold on. Just hold on." Before he lost control completely, he reached down for his jeans, dug into the pocket and pulled out the condoms he'd tucked in there only that morning.

"Boy," she said, "I really love a man who's prepared to take a nap."

He grinned at her as he sheathed himself. "Babe, ever since the moment we met, I've been prepared to nap."

"So glad to hear it." She opened her arms to him, lifted her hips again and welcomed him inside her.

That first slick, hot slide into her body stole his breath and would have finished him completely if he hadn't fought for control and held on to it. She moved into him, and the slippery threads of control fell away.

Together they climbed, staring into each other's eyes as they rode the crest of what they created. Mouths mating, breath mingling, they moved in an ancient dance as if they were born to be one. Together, they raced toward completion and together, they fell from the precipice, wrapped in each other's arms.

What could have been minutes or hours later, when breathing was easier, Rita cupped his face in her palm and whispered, "I hope you're still as sleepy as I am. Because I think I need another nap."

He turned his face into her palm, kissed it, then grinned down at her. "It's important to get enough sleep."

Jack groaned tightly as the memory faded and he was alone again in a room that suddenly felt too small, too quiet. Too empty.

He could still feel her small hand on his face, see her smile, taste her kiss. His body was tight, hard, eager. His mind raced with possibilities, before he shut them all down and accepted the cold reality.

Jack had a penance to pay and being this close to Rita without touching her was only the latest toll to be taken.

Jumping out of bed, he stalked through the open doors to the terrace and there he stood, letting the icy wind off the sea blow away the lingering heat still haunting him.

The next few days weren't easy.

Rita had to acknowledge that finding her way to the real Jack was going to be far more difficult than she'd anticipated. She was gone before he woke in the morning, heading down to the bakery where she worked to stay busy enough to keep thoughts of Jack at bay. Then in the evening, Jack did his best to avoid her completely. It was as if she was an unwanted guest he was trying to convince to leave.

Okay, yes, she'd agreed to a temporary marriage, but only because she'd caught those glimpses of *her* Jack. And now, he seemed determined to not let that happen again. He was pushing her away and expected her to simply give up and go when their time together was up.

"Well," she muttered to herself, "I'm not that easy to get rid of."

"Glad to hear it."

Rita closed her eyes, groaned quietly at being overheard—and by Jack's sister no less—then turned to face Cass. "Hi."

"Hi," the other woman said, walking farther into the kitchen. "I didn't mean to eavesdrop, but you were talking out loud so it was hard to miss."

"Sometimes," Rita admitted sheepishly, "I have to talk to myself because I'm the only one who really understands me."

Cass laughed. "Boy, I know that feeling. Between my practice, my husband and my kids, sometimes I talk to myself just to make sure I'm still there."

Rita relaxed her defenses a little. She'd liked Cass immediately when they'd met at the wedding. And listening to her now, Rita realized that with time, the two of them could be good friends. The question was, would she have that time?

"Look, I hope it's okay that I'm back here. The redhead out front said I could come in."

Casey again. "Of course it's okay. Have a seat. I'm just getting these loaves of bread ready for the ovens."

"God, it smells wonderful in here." Cass took a deep breath and sighed as she pulled a stool up to the marble work surface. Glancing around the room at the trays, the racks of cooling biscotti, bread and cannoli shells, she sighed. "Bread, cookies... I could live here."

Rita laughed and ran the blade of her knife along the elongated loaves of bread, making a few slices to give the dough room to grow while baking. "I love being in the kitchen."

"Well, clearly you have the talent for it," Cass said on a heavy sigh. "My husband has banned me from ours. He says what I call cooking, modern science calls poison."

"Oh, ouch."

Cass shrugged. "Yeah, it would be painful if

it weren't true. So we have a cook and everyone's happy."

She looked at a tray of thumbprint cookies with
their glossy chocolate centers and sighed again.
"Can I have one?"

"Sure."

She bit in. "Wow. Just wow."

Rita laughed and said, "Thank you."

"Oh, my pleasure." Cass watched her as she
readied the bread loaves and the silence spun out
for several seconds before she finally blurted out
the reason for her visit. "I'm really happy you
married Jack."

Oh, Rita hated guilt. She'd grown up Italian
Catholic and nobody did guilt better than they
did. Her mother was a master at making her kids
feel guilty and so Rita recognized the sensation
when it slapped her. She'd lied to her family. To
Jack's family.

Maybe even to herself, it was too soon to tell.
"Cass..."

The other woman waved one hand and shook
her head. "No, you don't have to say anything. I

just mean, I wanted to let you know that we're all glad he has someone. Jack's been…sort of shut down since he came home from his last tour."

Rita watched her, unsure what to say, or even what she *could* say.

"We've all tried to get through, but it's like trying to catch fog. Every time you think you're making progress, or maybe you see a flash of the old Jack, boom. It's gone." She shook her head and unconsciously reached for another cookie. Taking a bite, she sighed a little and continued. "If our mom was still alive, she'd have pushed past whatever boundaries he's got set up inside him. She wouldn't have accepted anything less."

Rita heard the wistful tone and responded. "She was tough?"

"When it came to her family? Oh, yeah." Cass grinned. "No one could stand in her way. But she's been gone five years and it's like the rest of us can't figure out how to reach Jack." She crumbled the rest of the cookie in her fingers. "That's why we're so glad he's got you. And the baby."

Oh, that guilt was really starting to get heavy,

Rita thought. What would Cass and the rest of their family think of Rita when this three-month marriage ended? Would they blame her for walking out on Jack, never knowing the real reason behind it?

"The worst part for me is I hate seeing my dad look so…helpless over this," Cass said. "He tries to talk to Jack but just can't and he's scared. Heck, we all are."

So was Rita. In the time since Jack had walked back into her life, she'd seen him withdraw not only from her but from the family who clearly loved him. Their marriage hadn't helped. If anything, he was working even harder at avoiding her.

"I don't like feeling helpless," Cass muttered. "I'm not good at it."

Rita smiled. Here, she really could bond with Cass. "Neither am I."

"Good." Cass gave her a conspiratorial smile. "I'm glad to hear it. That means you'll push him as maybe the rest of us can't."

But no pressure, Rita thought.

Six

Rita had a sister of her own and two older brothers, so she knew what it was to worry about a sibling. To want to help and not be allowed to. She could understand what Cass was feeling; Rita just didn't know if she was going to be able to do what the Buchanan family hoped she could. Bring Jack back to them.

"I don't know if Jack told you, but I'm a doctor."

She came up out of her thoughts with a jerk. "He did mention that. Family practice, right?"

"Right. Well, speaking as a doctor, not a sister," Cass said, "I can tell you that Jack's being affected by PTSD, which you've probably already guessed."

Rita nodded.

"There are so many different levels of this syndrome," Cass said with a sigh. "I've done a lot of reading and studying on it since Jack got home. And I know that the men and women affected by it are all different, so what they go through is different, as well. Naturally, treating it is a bitch. No one can find a standard type of treatment because each case is so wildly dissimilar."

Rita had come to that conclusion on her own. And it made perfect sense, really. Obviously, something horrible had happened to Jack on his last tour. When he left her six months ago, it was with a promise of a future that had been unsaid, but felt by both of them. And he'd come home for good just two months later, a completely changed man.

"I actually don't like the PTSD label—the word *disorder* bothers me. *Post-traumatic stress* I can get behind. But *disorder*? No." Cass shook her head firmly and scowled at what was left of her cookie. "That makes these men and women seem…sick, somehow. When what they are is *hurt*." She glanced up at Rita and winced. "Sorry. I didn't even realize I was climbing onto my soapbox."

Rita studied her for a minute or two. Not only was she a doctor, but she was the very concerned sister of a man suffering silently. "No apology necessary. I agree with you."

"Good. Thanks." Cass ate what was left of the cookie. "I knew at the wedding that I'd like you. And if you can help Jack through this, I'll love you forever."

Rita's heart opened up for the other woman. If one of her own brothers was in pain, she would do anything in her power, ask anyone she could think of, to get him the help he needed. Knowing that the Buchanans, in spite of all their money and power and influence, were as close as her own family made her feel more on solid ground. She could understand the driving need to save family and she liked Cass more for what she'd just confessed. "I'm going to try."

Cass smiled. "That's all we can do."

Rita walked to the wall ovens, opened the doors, then slid the bread trays inside, closed the doors and set the timers. As she wiped down the gray-streaked white marble counter, she asked, "Would you like a cup of coffee?"

"I'd *love* one," Cass said. "If you'll join me."

"No coffee for me yet," she said sadly, giving her baby bump a gentle rub. "But I'll have some herbal tea and cookies."

"That works." Cass grinned a little. "You know, if you haven't already lined up a pediatrician, I'd love to be your baby doctor."

Since she really hadn't chosen a doctor yet, this was a gift. "Who could be better than my baby's aunt?"

With Cass's beaming smile lighting her way, Rita walked to the front of the shop for the tea and coffee. Whatever else had happened today, she hoped she'd made a friend.

"Your wife is here," Linda announced over the intercom the very next afternoon.

"What?" Jack looked up from the file he was going over. "Rita?"

"Do you have another wife I don't know about yet?" Rita asked, sailing into the office with a wide smile on her face. "Thanks, Linda," she threw over her shoulder as Jack's assistant grinned, backed out of the office and shut the door.

Rita wore jeans, a white dress shirt and a black sweater over it that matched the black boots on her feet. Her brown curly hair was loose and tumbling around her face. Her brown eyes were shining and that smile pulled him in even as he fought against the draw.

"What're you doing here?" he asked as she walked through a slant of sunlight pouring through the windows to approach his desk.

"Such a warm welcome. Thanks. I'm glad to see you, too."

He frowned at the jab and her grin widened in response.

"I brought lunch," she said simply and held up

the dark green cloth bag he hadn't even noticed until that moment.

Just when he thought he'd figured out how to survive this marriage, she threw a wrench into the whole thing.

Every morning, he drove her to the bakery because damned if she was going to be driving herself through the darkness. Once she was safely inside, he drove back to the office and caught up on the dreaded paperwork that seemed to be what most of his days were made of. At the end of the day, he most often tried to just grab something for dinner and then disappear into his office or his bedroom. Jack knew the only way he was going to make it through the next three months was to keep as much distance between him and Rita as possible.

Damned hard though when she fought him at every turn. She insisted on breakfast at four in the morning. When he could, he avoided having dinner with her and simply escaped into his room or his office and stayed there until she was in bed.

He was living like a fugitive in his own damn apartment. And now, she'd hunted him down at work.

"Nice idea, but—"

"I called Linda to check," Rita said, interrupting him neatly as she began to empty that bag onto a table set between two overstuffed leather chairs. "She assured me your next appointment wasn't for two hours, so we have plenty of time for lunch."

He bit back a curse. What good would it do at this point? Sometimes, he reminded himself, surrender was your only option. "What've you got?" he asked.

She flipped her hair back, turned her head to smile at him. "I went to your favorite Chinese place. I've got beef and broccoli, chicken chow mein and shrimp fried rice."

As she opened cartons to spoon the food onto two plates she pulled from her bag, Jack took a breath and drew in the delicious scents. Well, hell, he had to eat sometime, right?

He pushed up from the desk and walked across

the room, took one of the chairs and accepted the plate Rita handed him. She grinned at him and his insides rolled over. The woman had power over him, for sure. He was achy and needy most of the time now and he had her to thank for it. Her image was always in his mind. The hunger for her never eased. And having her in his house and still untouchable was harder than he even imagined it would be.

Jack was starting to think she was deliberately trying to seduce him just by acting as though nothing was going on between them. And damned if it wasn't working.

"Think you're pretty clever, don't you?"

"Absolutely," she agreed, and sat down in the chair opposite him. She dug into the bag again, and came up with two bottles of water, two sets of chopsticks and a stack of napkins.

"So," she said, "how're things in the megabusiness world?"

The food looked delicious and smelled amazing. He took a bite, savored it, then said, "Buying, selling. How's the bakery?"

She shrugged. "Measuring, mixing, baking."

Her eyes were shining, her smile was hypnotic and she smelled even better than the food. Jack was on dangerous ground already. Having her invade the office he thought of as his own personal cave wasn't helping anything. Now he'd be seeing her here, even when she wasn't. There had to be boundaries. For everyone's sake.

"Why're you really here?" he asked. "Isn't the bakery busy enough for you?"

"Oh, it really is. But Casey's a great manager." She took a sip of water. "As you said yourself, I'm the boss, I can take a break when I want to."

Tough having your own words thrown back at you and used against you.

"I can't," he said, but he kept eating the chow mein. It really was good. "Look, I appreciate this, but it's not something that should become a habit."

"Really?" She tipped her head to one side. "Why not?"

"Because we both have work," he said and knew it sounded lame. But off the cuff it was the best he had.

"Uh-huh." Thoughtfully, she took another bite of her broccoli, then asked, "Sure it's not because you're trying to avoid being around me?"

"If that were true," he countered, "why would I have married you?"

"Such a good question." She took another bite. "Have an answer?"

This was not going well. He was losing a battle he hadn't even been aware he'd entered. "You know why we got married."

"The baby."

"Exactly. This wasn't about us having lunch or dinner together," he pointed out, but hadn't stopped eating yet. "This isn't about cozy nights at home, Rita, and you know it. It's an arrangement with an expiration date."

"Hmm. And, it wasn't about you driving me to work every morning either and yet..." She shrugged again, a small smile tugging at the corner of her mouth.

Well, he'd stepped right into that one.

"That's different," he argued. "You used to

live above the bakery now you have to drive to work—"

"Six miles," she threw in.

"This isn't about the distance, it's about safety." He took a drink of water. "I'm not letting you drive through the city alone in the middle of the night when it's just as easy for me to drive you."

"So you're worried about my safety. That doesn't sound disinterested to me," she mused, taking another bite.

"Being concerned doesn't mean worried." Though he was. Hell, the thought of her driving alone through the city in the middle of the night gave him chills. What if she got a flat tire? Or the car just died? Or something happened with the baby?

She took another bite and watched him as she chewed and swallowed. Sunlight filtered through the windows and made her dark hair shine with golden highlights. Just watching her chew had his body going on red alert. It was that mouth, he told himself. That full, generous, completely kissable mouth that was doing him in.

"You work so hard to pretend that you're oblivious to me and your family, but it's not working."

His frown deepened and rather than argue, he took another bite of his lunch.

"Look it up in a dictionary, Jack. *Concerned* means *worried*. And that's exactly what you are. Worried, I mean. Oh, don't say anything," she said, waving her chopsticks when he started to deny it, "I know it bothers you to be worried, so that's almost the same as not being, unless you think about it carefully and then it's exactly the same thing and you don't want to recognize that, do you?"

Jack stared at her. "What?"

Shaking her head she took a sip of water, "Nothing, never mind. Doesn't matter right now. I didn't get the chance to tell you, but your sister came to the bakery to see me yesterday."

His head snapped up. Suddenly, her conversation was taking several different paths at once and none of them were making sense. "Cass?"

"You have two sisters as well as two wives?" she asked, teasing.

"Funny." That smile was really hard to resist and he was pretty sure she knew it since she kept flashing it at him.

"A little, maybe." She shrugged again. "Anyway, Cass wanted to talk about you, big surprise."

Well, there went the appetite. He set his plate aside, reached for his water and took a long drink. "That's what this visit is about then," he said. "What Cass had to say."

"Nope." She shook her head, sending those brown curls into a wild dance that made him want to spear his fingers through them. "I was coming to surprise you anyway. This just gives us more to talk about."

"No, thanks." He took another drink, half wishing it was a beer. "I'm not interested in conversations and besides, I have to get back to work."

"No you don't," she said, setting her plate aside, too. "You're just trying to get rid of me again."

"Again?"

She sighed. "Jack, you avoid me every chance you get. The penthouse is big, but not so big that we shouldn't run into each other more often. But you see to it that we don't." She ran one hand lovingly over her baby bump, but her gaze never left his. "Even when I trap you into breakfast in the morning, you just bolt it down and dodge every attempt at conversation."

"Four thirty in the morning, not the best time for chats."

"What's your excuse then for dinner?" Still shaking her head, she said, "Usually, you grab an apple or something and disappear into your office. Or if you do sit down with me, we don't talk. Heck, you hardly look at me directly."

It was too damn hard to look at her. To want her so badly it was a constant, driving ache inside. He was paying, daily. His atonement continued and he could only hope that he survived it somehow.

"Rita…"

"Your family's worried about you."

He scraped both hands across his face, then stood up, unable to sit still any longer. "You don't have to tell me about my own family."

"Are you sure?" She stood up, too, and faced him, toe-to-toe. A part of him admired that spine of hers. He'd liked it right off, from the moment they met and she hadn't been afraid. But right now, he wished she was more cautious, less ready for a confrontation.

"They want to help you and they don't know how," she said. "*I* don't know how."

"I didn't ask for help," he reminded her tautly. "I can deal with things my own way."

"Not so far," she countered and folded her arms across her middle.

His eyes narrowed on her. "You don't know anything about it."

"Then *tell* me," she challenged, moving closer, tipping her head back to meet his eyes. "And if not me, Jack, tell *someone.*"

"Therapy?" He laughed, shook his head and shoved one hand through his hair. "Yeah, not needing a couch, or some stranger poking around in my head. No, thanks."

"Tough marine doesn't need anyone, is that it?"

He glanced at her, read frustration clearly in her eyes but there was nothing he could do about it. "Close enough."

"Well, you're wrong, Jack," she said and this time when she moved closer, she laid one hand on his chest, right over his heart. Silently, he wondered if she felt the staccato beat beneath her palm. If she had the slightest clue what she did to him.

"Even marines are human, Jack. Even marines can't fix everything solo." She stared up into his eyes and he was unable to look away. "People need each other. That's why we *have* families, Jack. Because we're stronger together. Because we can count on each other when things get hard."

He ground his teeth together and fought for patience. He knew she meant well. Hell, he knew they *all* meant well. But they couldn't help unless he talked and he wasn't going to talk about it. About any of it.

Through gritted teeth, he said softly, "I'm fine, Rita."

"Yeah, I can see that," she said. "That's why you don't have to set an alarm to get up at four a.m., because you can't sleep but you're fine."

He jerked his head back to give her a glare. "How the hell do you know I can't sleep?"

"I can hear you, moving around the apartment, going out onto the terrace…"

Apparently, he wasn't as stealthy as he liked to think. And he had to ask himself, if he'd known she was awake, too, would he have gone to her? Tried to lose himself and the dreams that dogged him in the warmth of her embrace? Would he have given in to the insistent urge to take her, to find the heat and the welcome he'd once found in her arms? He didn't know the answer and that worried him.

"Sorry," he said tightly, rubbing the back of his neck. "I'll be quieter."

"Oh, Jack, that's not what I meant at all," she said and rested her hand on his forearm. "I'm right here. Let me in. Am I so scary you can't talk to me?"

For the first time ever, he was tempted to do just that. To just start talking and in the talking, maybe the images in his head would start to fade. Looking down into those compelling eyes of hers, he could feel himself weakening, in spite of the promise he'd made to himself. That he would never talk about the past, because doing that kept it alive. Kept it vivid. But hadn't it stayed alive despite his silence?

"I'm not going to do that." He shook his head and gave a halfhearted laugh. "Besides, one thing you're not, Rita, is scary."

"I can be, when pushed. Just ask my brothers."

Gaze still locked with hers, he lifted one hand, smoothed her hair back and briefly let himself enjoy the silky feel of it against his skin. Her emotions crowded those whiskey-brown eyes of hers and her teeth tugged at her bottom lip. God, she was beautiful. He wished...

"Let it be, Rita," he said quietly. "Just let it be."

"You know I can't."

She stared up at him and he fisted his hands at his sides to keep from grabbing her, burying his face in the curve of her neck and drawing her scent deep inside him. She made him feel too much and he couldn't allow that. He was done with caring. Done with letting others care about him. It was the safest way.

Finally, she lifted both hands and cupped his face in her palms. Heat from her body poured into his and still couldn't thaw the knot of ice he carried deep inside. "Rita, just leave my secrets in the past. Where they belong."

Looking deeply into his eyes, Rita shook her head. "They're not staying in the past, Jack. They're right here, surrounding you, cutting you off from me. From everyone. So no, I won't let it be. Not a chance."

Rita couldn't sleep. Maybe it was the confrontation/lunch with Jack two days before. Maybe it was the baby, who had decided to start training as a gymnast while still in the womb. And maybe it was just the whirring sounds of her own thoughts spinning frantically in her mind. Whatever it was, though, pulled her from bed and sent her pacing the penthouse.

It was beautiful, she had to admit, though it was a little impersonal for her. Beige walls, gleaming wood floors and comfortable, if boring, furniture. There were generic paintings on the walls and in the penthouse kitchen, the appliances were top-of-the-line, but the dishware was buy-a-box-of-plates-style.

Nothing in the place spoke of Jack. It was as if some decorator had come in, put in inoffensive furniture and left it at that, expecting whoever lived there to eventually make it their own. But apparently Jack had no interest in putting his own stamp on the place. Here, like everywhere else in his life, he was simply an observer. As if he were a placeholder for the real person who hadn't arrived yet.

Rita curled up on the forest green couch, pulled a throw pillow onto her lap and wrapped her arms around it.

For two days, she'd been determined to make Jack interact with her. She refused to let him lock himself away in his office once he returned to the penthouse. She made dinner and forced him to talk to her over a meal. She told him all about what was happening at the bakery and peppered him with questions about his work.

She didn't understand half of what he was talking about—with cargo containers and shipping schedules, but at least he was talking. She asked questions about his family and listened when he told her stories from his childhood, the fishing trips, the cabin they used to have in Big Bear.

And though she was managing to keep him engaged, it was a lot of work. The man spoke grudgingly and she had to practically drag information from him. But it was better than letting him brood alone. Still, her heart hurt because she wasn't getting to him. She wasn't any closer now to finding the real Jack than she had been when she married him.

Moonlight pearled the darkness. If she'd had company, it might have been romantic. As it was, though, she felt sad and tired and frustrated all at once.

"If he doesn't care, why is he working so hard to shut me out?" she asked the empty room and her voice sounded overly loud in the quiet. Hugging the pillow a little tighter to her middle, she told herself that if he didn't care about her or their baby, he wouldn't have so much trouble being around her.

"And if that doesn't sound backward I don't know what does." But it made an odd kind of sense, too. He was throwing himself on a pro-verbial sword by avoiding her. Making sacrifices she didn't want for a reason he wouldn't share.

So how was she supposed to fight it?

The week she'd spent with him now seemed like a dream. Even that last morning in her hotel room had taken on the soft edges of a fantasy rather than the warm, loving reality she remembered.

"I should go," Jack said, bending his head to take her mouth in a kiss that was filled with a hunger that never seemed to ebb.

"Not yet." Rita cupped his cheek in her palm and looked into those amazing blue eyes, trying to etch everything she read there into her memory. "Stay. Just for a while."

He smiled and threaded his fingers through her hair. Rita closed her eyes briefly to completely savor the sensation of his hands on her. She'd never known a week to fly by so quickly. She'd thought only to take a week at the beach. A little vacation to clear her head after the Christmas holiday rush at the bakery back home.

But she'd found so much more than she'd ever expected. A man who made her laugh, made her sigh and made her body sing in a way she'd never known before. They'd spent every waking moment together in the last few days and even asleep, they were locked together as if somehow afraid of being separated.

And now, they would be.

Her heart was breaking at goodbye. But her flight home was that night and Jack would be leaving himself first thing in the morning. Their time was up. But what did that mean for the future?

"My enlistment's nearly up," he was saying and she told herself to concentrate on the low rumble of his voice. "This time, I'm not going to re-up. I'm getting out."

She ran her hand over his chest, loving the feel

of those sharply defined muscles beneath soft, golden-brown skin. "What's that mean for us?"

He slid one hand up the length of her body to cup her breast, his thumb and forefinger tugging on her hardened nipple. Electricity zipped through her entire body and set up a humming expectation at the very core of her. One touch from this man and she was a puddle of goo at his feet.

"It means I can come up to Utah as soon as I get home."

"Good," she said on a sigh. "That's very good."

"And we'll pick this up," he said, "right where we left off."

"Even better," she said and got a smile from him. "Please be careful, Jack."

She could have bitten her own tongue off. She'd promised herself she wouldn't cry. Wouldn't worry him. Wouldn't put her own worries onto his shoulders.

"I will be," he promised. "Always am. But this time, I've got even more reason for making it home in one piece."

He was smiling as he said it, but fear nearly

choked her. Rita reached up, wrapped her arms around his neck and held on, as if somehow if she held him tightly enough, she could keep him safe. Keep him from going. From leaving her. Tears stung the backs of her eyes, but she blinked like a crazy person, to keep them at bay.

She didn't want to let him see her cry.

"Hey," he soothed, rubbing his hand up and down her arm for comfort. "I'll be okay. I swear it."

She nodded into his chest, but kept her face buried against him so he wouldn't read her fear on her face.

"Rita," he said, and gently moved her head back so he could look down into her eyes. "I swear to you. I'll be back. And I'll come to you."

"You'd better," she quipped, trying to take the pain out of goodbye. "I have two older brothers who will beat you up if I ask them to."

"Well, now I'm scared." He grinned, kissed her again, running his tongue over her lips until she parted them, sighing at the invasion of her mouth. When he had her completely stirred up, he pulled

back again. "I never thought to find someone like you, Rita. Trust me when I say I don't want to lose you."

"I'm glad. I don't want to lose you, either, Jack."

"You won't."

Late-afternoon sunlight spilled into the room and bathed the two of them in a golden haze. A soft, cool breeze ruffled the curtains hanging at the partially opened window.

Letting his gaze sweep up and down her body, he finally met her eyes again and whispered, "You are the best thing that's ever happened to me, Rita. Never forget that."

Oh, God. That sounded too final and she couldn't accept that. He had to come home. To her. So she smiled and fought for courage.

"Don't you forget it, either," she said.

"Not a chance."

He kissed her again and she knew it was good-bye. He had to leave. See his family before shipping out in the morning. And she had a flight to Utah to catch.

When he slid off the bed and grabbed his jeans,

she sat up, dragging the coverlet up to cover her breasts. Pushing her hair back out of her eyes, she watched him dress and her mouth went dry.

"You'll write to me," she said, not a question.

"I will." He patted the pocket of his shirt. "I've got your address and you'll have mine as soon as you get a letter from me. I'd give it to you now, but I can't be sure it won't change. Hell, I'm not even sure my email address will be the same."

"Doesn't matter." She shook her head, went up on her knees and reached for him. He held her close and she locked her arms around his waist, resting her head on his chest. She heard the steady beat of his heart and prayed it would remain safe and steady until she was with him again. "Just write to me, Jack. And let me know you're safe."

He tipped her chin up with the tips of his fingers. "And when I'm coming home."

"That, too." He kissed her again, looked long and deep into her eyes, then turned for the door. At the threshold, he paused, turned back and sighed. "You take my breath away."

She covered her mouth with one hand and knew she would soon lose the battle with her tears. "Be safe, Jack. And come home to me."

He gave her a sharp nod, then turned and left, the door closing quietly behind him. Alone, Rita walked to the window, the coverlet a toga of sorts, around her naked body. She pulled the edges of the curtains back, looked down into the parking lot and saw him, taking long, sure strides toward his black Jeep.

As if he could sense her watching him, he turned, looked up at her and simply held her gaze for several long seconds. Then he got in the car and drove away.

But he never wrote. He never came to her. If she hadn't moved to Long Beach to feel closer to a memory, she might never have known he was even alive. Was that Fate blessing them? Or cursing them?

"Down! Get down!"

Startled at the muffled shout, Rita jumped to her feet and whipped her head around to stare at the darkened hall leading to Jack's bedroom.

Starting down the hall, the wood floor was cold against her bare feet. With every step she took, his voice came louder, more desperate.

She ran, following his shouts, his pain.

Her heart.

Seven

Jack shouted himself awake, jolted upright in bed and struggled to breathe. The dream—*nightmare*—still held him in a tightfisted grip and he had to force himself to look around the moonlit room to orient himself. He was home, yet his heart still raced and his mouth and throat were dry. A black duvet pooled in his lap, his bare chest was covered in sweat and his gaze was wild. He scrubbed one hand across his face, rubbing his eyes as if he could wipe away the fear raised by the images still stamped in his mind.

"Jack? Jack, are you okay?" Rita hurried into the room.

"I'm fine," he muttered thickly, jumping out of bed. *Perfect. Just perfect.* He'd woken her up and now she'd stare at him with either pity or fear and he didn't think he could take either.

He wore loosely tied cotton pants that dipped low on his hips and he was grateful he'd decided not to sleep naked since she'd moved in. Damn it. Jack needed a little time to get a grip. To shove those memories back into the dark corner of his mind where they were usually locked away. He needed to be clearheaded when he talked to Rita. Jack just didn't see that happening anytime soon.

He pushed one hand through his hair and looked at her as if she were a mirage. Jack had pulled himself out of a hot, dusty dream where the sound of explosions and gunfire still echoed in the stillness around him. Seeing her here, in the dark moon-washed confines of his bedroom, a world away from the scene that still haunted him, was almost too much to compute. "Sorry I woke you. Just…go back to sleep."

He turned his back on her, hoping to hell she'd leave, and walked out onto the terrace, welcoming the brisk slap of wind. Sea spray scented the air that he dragged into his lungs, to replace the dry dustiness that felt as though it was coating him in more than memories.

"Jack?"

Damn.

She'd followed him onto the terrace and the touch of her hand against his bare back had him flinching. Every nerve in his body was firing, on alert.

"What is it?" She stood right behind him, her voice soft, low, soothing. "*Talk* to me."

He whipped his head around to glare at her. "I don't want to talk. That should be clear. Just leave me alone, Rita. You don't want to be with me right now."

"Yeah," she insisted and didn't look the least bit cowed. "I do. Or I wouldn't be here."

Gritting his teeth, Jack ground out tightly, "I'm on the ragged edge here, Rita. I need some space."

"No, you don't."

He choked out a harsh laugh. "Is that right? And you're an expert on me, is that it?"

"Enough to know that you've had enough space," she countered, stepping in closer. "Too much, maybe. Everyone backs off when you tell them to, but I won't. I'm here, Jack, and I'm not going anywhere. You can't use a nasty tone and a miserable attitude to shake me off. *Talk* to me."

His skin was buzzing, his mind racing and his heartbeat was still at a fast gallop. Jack had come out of that damn dream ready to fight, but there was no enemy to face. He needed to move. To fight. To do *something*, to expel the ghosts gathered around him, shrieking for his attention.

"Damn it, Jack," Rita said, tugging at his forearm until he turned to face her again. Her whiskey eyes were hot, burning with passion and fury and he wasn't sure which had top billing.

"I'm not deaf or blind," she said. "I heard you shouting. I stepped into your room in time to see you bolt up in bed as if the hounds of hell were after you."

She'd hit that one on the head. Scraping one hand over his face, he muttered, "They were."

"Then tell me." She held on to him, the heat of her touch sliding into his arm, moving through his bloodstream. "Let me in, damn it. What does it cost you to open the door just a crack?"

He speared her with a hard look. There was no pity, no fear in her eyes. Only concern and curiosity and maybe that was worse in some ways.

"You think it's *me* I'm worried about?" He grabbed her shoulders, giving her a little shake for emphasis. "It's *you* I'm thinking about here. I'm trying to save you, don't you get it?"

"Save me? From what?"

"God, you won't let this go," he muttered thickly.

"Not a chance."

He stared into her eyes. "Fine. I'm trying to save you from me. Okay? I don't even trust myself around you right now."

"That's ridiculous."

There was a response he hadn't expected.

"You're not trying to injure me in some way,

Jack," she pointed out, her voice a little louder, her eyes a little more fiery. "You've done your best to simply avoid me at all costs."

"There's a reason—"

"Did I ask you to save me?" she interrupted, breaking free of his grip. The cold ocean air lifted her hair into a cloud of dark curls around her head and with the flash in her eyes, she looked like a pagan goddess. Even the nightgown she wore that was hot-pink with the image of a cupcake on it and the words *SWEET THING* scrawled across the top couldn't diminish her. No, not a goddess, he corrected. Instead, she looked like a short, Italian Valkyrie. She was furious and her eyes were shot with sparks.

She poked her index finger into the center of his chest. "I'm a big girl. I save myself when I need it. I don't need a knight in shining armor, Jack." She shoved her hair out of her eyes impatiently. "What I need is for my *husband* to tell me what's tearing at him."

"You would have made a great warrior, Rita," he said softly, gaze raking her up and down, from her bare toes with their purple-polished nails up to the eyes that were so incensed he was surprised she wasn't actually shooting flames from them. "You are a Fury, aren't you? Not afraid of anything."

"Not afraid of *you*, anyway," she said, whipping her head back to shake her hair free of her eyes.

How the hell was a man supposed to win an argument with a woman like this? How was he supposed to ignore her, ignore what she made him feel?

"Maybe you should be," he said, pulling her in close with one quick move. "And if I were a better man, I'd tell you to leave. Now. But I'm not—so if you want to run, now's your chance."

She reached up, cupped his face in her palms and demanded, "Does it look like I'm going anywhere?"

"No. Thank God." He bent his head, and took her mouth in a kiss that was filled with the hunger and desperation he'd felt since she reentered his life.

With the dregs of the nightmare still clinging

to him, Jack held her tighter, his hands running up and down her back and down to her bottom. He pulled her against his rock-hard body and she wriggled closer in appreciation. Expectation. His blood ran hot and fast, his heartbeat raced and his mind was fogged by the want choking him. *Need* was alive and shouting inside him.

The cold ocean wind wrapped itself around them, but he didn't feel it. Nothing could vanquish the internal heat. One hand cupped the back of her head and held her still so he could completely claim her mouth. His tongue tangled with hers and her eager response fed the flames licking at his soul.

There was no time for romance, seduction. He needed to be with her. In her. Over her. Tearing his mouth from hers, he looked down into her now-glassy eyes and fought to breathe.

"What're you doing?" she managed to ask breathlessly. "Why are you stopping?"

"Not stopping. Changing location." He bent down, scooped her up and carried her back through the French doors and into his bedroom.

Moonlight followed them, the wind rushed in behind them and none of that mattered. He laid her down on the mattress and, in one deft move, stripped her nightgown off, leaving her naked—just as he wanted her. She scooted back farther on the mattress and reached for him. Jack didn't keep her waiting. He yanked off the sleep pants he was wearing and joined her on the bed an instant later. His hands moved over her, exploring every curve. Every line.

He remembered this so well. Had tormented himself over the last few months, by recalling the feel of her skin, the lush fullness of her breasts and the taut, dark nipples that he loved to suckle.

And now, because of the baby, she was so much more than she had been. She was ripe, delectable and more alluring than ever. Even as he thought it, though, both of her hands went to the mound of her belly as if to hide it from him. He drew her hands away and said, "Don't. You're beautiful."

She laughed. "I'm huge."

He shook his head. "No. Curvy. Delicious. Amazing."

She sighed a little. "Wow. When you try, you really know the right things to say."

He grinned, bent his head and indulged himself in what he'd wanted to do for weeks now. He took one nipple into his mouth and savored the taste of her. Her scent invaded him, the soft sighs and moans sliding from her throat enflamed him. He ran his tongue and teeth across the tip of her nipple and then suckled, drawing her very essence into himself.

She planted her feet on the mattress and lifted her hips. "Touch me, Jack. Touch me."

He did. Sweeping one hand down the length of her body, he cupped her center and used his thumb to brush across her most sensitive spot. She jerked beneath him and he smiled against her breast, relishing her reaction. He suckled harder, and then lifted his head to switch to her other breast and she went crazy in his arms. As if the need that had been building between them for weeks had finally reached a breaking point for both of them, she rocked her hips into his hand.

He pushed two fingers into her heat and groaned himself at the slick, tight feel of her. It had been too long. His body was ready to explode and so was hers. He couldn't wait another minute to be inside her, to feel her body surrounding his.

Lifting his head, he looked down at her then kissed her briefly. "At least we don't need a condom now."

"Points for us," she said, swallowing hard, breath coming in short, hard gasps. "Damn it, Jack, don't drag this out. I need you inside me."

"Just what I need, too," he said, and shifted position to kneel between her thighs. He spread her legs wide and looked down at her. She was wanton, wild and everything he'd ever wanted in a woman. And for this one moment at least, she was his again—as she was always meant to be.

His mind whispered that this was temporary. That this marriage wasn't real and he was nobody's idea of husband material anyway. But he shut that nagging voice down and surrendered to the mating call trumpeting through his body.

He ran his hands over her hot, slick center,

watching her twist and writhe in her own desperate need.

Her response pushed his own desires beyond what he could bear. Body throbbing, heart galloping, he leaned over her and pushed himself inside her. That first, glorious slide filled him with the kind of ease he hadn't known in months. This was what had been missing in his life. This sense of rightness that claimed him when their bodies were joined.

She hooked her legs at his hips and pulled him in tighter, deeper. Tipping her head back into the mattress, she bit her lip and moved with him. Their bodies meshed, linked in the most intimate way possible, he felt the pounding of her heart. Saw the flash in her eyes, heard her gasping breaths and experienced her body quaking, quivering as he pushed her higher, faster than they'd ever gone before.

Her nails scored his back as he rocked in and out of her body, setting a rhythm she raced to meet. "Jack! Jack!"

"Come on, Rita," He urged, barely able to frame

the words as his breath sawed in and out of his lungs. "Go over. Go over so I can follow."

She clung to him and shouted his name when the first tremors took her. He felt her body tighten around his in spasms of delight and when she'd reached her peak, Jack let go and found the peace that had been denied him for months.

Rita took some deep breaths and tried to ease the frantic beat of her heart at the same time. It had been six long months since he'd touched her like that. Time in which she'd almost convinced herself that her memory was making what they shared much better than it actually had been. Well, she told herself, *that* theory was just shot out of the sky.

Her whole body was so alight with sensation she thought she should glow in the dark. And even while she tried to regain control, she was thinking about doing it all again. She turned her head to look at Jack, lying beside her. One arm flung across his eyes, his chest heaved with every breath and she smiled, knowing that he was just as shaken as she. Had she finally broken through the wall he'd built around himself? Was her Jack finally back?

"You owe me twenty bucks," he said softly.

She blinked at him, then laughed. "Seriously? You want a *tip*?"

He lowered his arm and turned his gaze on her. "Nope. A bet we made. Not only did you marry me when you said you wouldn't, you just—"

She held up one hand. "I know what I just—" then she slapped both hands to her hips as if checking for a wallet "—I don't seem to have any pockets at the moment so I'll have to owe you."

One corner of his mouth quirked. "I suppose I can live with that."

Rolling to one side, he propped himself up on one elbow and looked down at her. "Rita—"

She stopped him by laying her fingers on his mouth. Disappointment welled in her chest. Looking into his eyes, she could see that her Jack was still buried behind a shutter of ice. Maybe there were a few cracks in that cold stillness, but it was a seductive stranger staring at her through Jack's eyes. Her heart hurt for it, but she wouldn't give up. Now more than ever, it was important to find a way to completely reach him.

"Don't you dare apologize for this," she said firmly. "*Or* tell me that it'll never happen again—"

He tried to speak, but she hurried on. "We both wanted this, Jack. And I want it again right now."

"Want isn't the point," he ground out as he laid one arm across her middle.

"Then what is?" She reached up and smoothed his hair back from his forehead, just because she wanted her fingers in that thick, wavy mass. Rita needed to touch him, to ground herself and hope-fully *him*. To remind them both that the threads binding them were still there. They hadn't been broken, only strained. She had to believe they could strengthen them again.

"Talk to me," she said, locking her gaze on his so that he could see how much she wanted this. That when he told his story, whatever it was, he would still be safe with her. "Tell me what you were dreaming. Why were you shouting? What made you grab hold of me and hang on like I was a lifeboat in a tsunami?"

He scowled, but she was so used to that expression now, it didn't even affect her. "I don't want to talk about it."

"Just dream about it then?" she countered, refusing to give up on him. *Them.* "Don't you see that if you do tell me, maybe it will make the dreams fade?"

"Nothing can."

Then the baby kicked and his features went blank with surprise. He glanced down to where his arm rested across her belly and then he sucked in a gulp of air when the baby kicked again, as if reminding its parents that they weren't alone. His astonished gaze snapped to hers. "That was—"

"A good kick," she finished for him. She knew what he was feeling, because she'd felt exactly the same the first time the baby'd moved. It was magic, she knew. Staggering. That tiny life making itself known. Taking his hand, she held it tightly to the mound of their child.

On cue, another kick came and Jack's eyes

went wide even as an unexpected grin lit his face. "Strong baby."

That wide smile of his tugged at her heart. "Like its father."

Just like that, his smile faded into memory. Pulling away from her grasp, he asked, "What is it? The baby, I mean. Do you know?"

If he hadn't pulled away from her, Rita would have thought that she was making more progress with him. He hadn't once asked about the baby before, so normally, she would have celebrated internally that he was feeling…linked. But the look in his eyes was cool, not warm, and so she had to admit that nothing had changed.

"No," she said sadly, sorry that he was withdrawing again. "I didn't want to know ahead of time. I wanted to be surprised. There aren't many real surprises left in the world."

"*You* always surprised me," he said. "Still do." Just for a second, she saw another crack in the wall around him. Then it was gone and as if to prove it to her, he turned and pushed off the bed.

He walked naked to the open French doors and

out onto the terrace. On the twenty-fifth floor, facing the ocean, there was no one to see them. No nosy neighbors.

He stood there in the cold wind, his hair lifted off his neck and Rita wanted to touch it, feel it against her skin again. Broad shoulders, narrow hips and long, muscular legs made her mouth water, but while her blood burned, her mind mourned because he was trying to pull away from her. Again.

But Rita wasn't going to let him. Not this time. Scrambling off the bed, she went to him and pulled at his upper arm until he turned to face her. "I'm not going to quit trying to reach you, Jack."

He shook his head. "Did you ever think that maybe there's nothing to reach?"

"No." She shook her head, too, just as fiercely determined to find him as he was to hide. "There's *you*, Jack. And I'm not going to stop pestering, pushing you. I'm not going to stop asking you what happened, so you might as well give in now and tell me."

"Damn, you've got a hard head," he murmured, with the faintest of smiles.

"That's been said before." She looked at him ruefully. "By *you*, mostly. Jack, tell me. Tell me what's haunting you."

He grimaced. "*Haunting* is the right word for it."

"Talk."

A harsh laugh that held no humor scraped his throat and his gaze swung past her to lock on the dark, roiling ocean. But he looked more as though he was focusing on something only he could see. His ghosts. His past. And finally, Rita thought, he was going to bring her into the shadows with him. Maybe then, she'd be able to hold his hand and lead him back into the light.

"You want to know?" He blew out a breath. "Fine. Here it is. Two days after I left you, I was back with my unit." He glanced at her briefly before turning his gaze to the sea. "I was actually writing you a letter when my squad was sent out to do some recon on a nearby village."

Her heartbeat stuttered a little, knowing that he

had been keeping his promise to write and a little fearful of what had kept him from completing that letter. Rita watched him, judging every tiny twist of his features, trying to guess at the turnings of his mind, at the nearness of his ghosts. Her gaze on his profile, she held her breath and waited.

His voice sounded far away as if he wasn't really there with her at all, but instead, he was caught in his memories. He was somehow more a part of his past than he was a part of his life, here. She had to know why.

"We were told there was sniper activity so we were careful. Well, thought we were." He shook his head, gritted his teeth and forced the words out. "I'm not going into details here, Rita. You don't need to know them anyway. Short version. One of my guys was shot. We took cover, a couple of men breaking right while my best friend and I went left, dragging the wounded man with us."

"Jack…" She put one hand on his forearm.

"There was an IED on the left."

Tears drenched her eyes. She didn't know what

was coming next, but her heart ached just looking at his stony profile, the hard set of his jaw,
his narrowed gaze.

"The wounded man was killed. My friend
Kevin got hit hard. His legs." He blew out a breath
then dragged in another gulp of the cold, sea air.
Shaking his head, he swallowed hard and continued, "Somehow, we got the sniper and then I
could work on Kevin's wounds. I got tourniquets
on him but he fought me." He paused, to steady
himself, to distance himself from the pain? She
couldn't know. But he kept talking, so she stayed
quiet.

"Kevin didn't want to live without his legs—
kept cursing at me to leave him be. I wouldn't
listen. Couldn't let him die."

"Of course not." God, to have such scenes and
more in your head. To see them in your sleep.
His sister, Cass, was right. These guys weren't
sick. They were hurt. Right down to their souls.
Rita wrapped her arms around him and held on
whether he was aware of her or not.

"We called for medics and evac. One guy dead,

two wounded and Kevin, half-conscious and still cursing me for saving him." Jack scrubbed one hand across his mouth as if he could somehow wipe away the taste of his own words. Then he finally shifted his gaze to hers and when she looked into his eyes, Rita felt the sympathy he'd already said he didn't want.

"I couldn't write to you after that," he said. "Couldn't even think about you. I talked to my friend's widow after they notified her and left her broken to pieces. She loved Mike so much that losing him shattered her completely. Then I went to see my best friend, Kevin, before they flew him out for surgery and he wouldn't even talk to me.

"Hell, he wouldn't *look* at me. All those curses he'd brought down on my head for saving him were still running through my head and probably his. It was like I was dead to him."

"You never talked to him again?"

"No." Jack took a breath and blew it out again. "He contacted me a couple of months ago, but I didn't get back to him."

"Why not?"

"What's the point, Rita?" He shoved both hands through his hair. "You think I want to stand there, look at him in a chair and have him ream me all over again? No, thanks."

She felt for him. He'd saved his friend, done his best for him and the man had fought him every step of the way. No wonder he was tortured by nightmares and didn't want to talk about what he remembered. But things might have changed for his friend by now. Maybe he wanted to make amends with Jack and by not allowing it, Jack kept the pain close and fresh.

"You don't know what he wanted," she told him. "Maybe he wanted to say thank you."

"I don't need to be thanked, either," he snapped. "I did what I had to do. That's it."

The emptiness in Jack's eyes was so profound, Rita didn't know how he could still be standing. He had to be the strongest man she'd ever known. And the most alone. Even with a family who loved him, a wife and a child on the way, he was so terribly alone.

Voice brisk, letting her know this little truth-telling session was now at an end, he said, "Anyway. After all that, I had nothing left for you, Rita." Shaking his head, he said softly, "Still don't. I'm not the guy you knew. Hell, I don't even recognize that man anymore."

"Well, I do," she said, going up on her toes to kiss him. "I know him. I still see him when I look into your eyes. And I know you're punishing yourself for something that wasn't your fault."

"My squad. My calls."

"And you think I have a hard head."

He glanced at her, surprise flickering in his eyes.

"Jack, you were ordered to check out that village. You all took cover. What happened, just… happened. You're not in charge of who lives and dies. Jack, you did the best you could."

"Wasn't good enough," he insisted.

"It was, because it was all you *could* do." Now that she knew, she could almost understand him cutting himself off from her, from his family, from everything that was important to him.

He'd seen too much loss. And he didn't want to
risk more of it. So by shutting down his heart, he
thought he was protecting himself. Instead, he'd
welcomed a different kind of pain. Rita laid her
head on his chest and listened to the wild thump-
ing of his heart. He stiffened against her and for
a second, she thought he was going to shove her
aside, but instead, he grabbed her tight, pulled her
closer. Buried his face in the curve of her neck.

"Damn it, Rita," he murmured, "you should
have left it alone."

"I can't do that, Jack. I can't leave *you* alone."
She wondered if he heard the love in her voice. If
he understood how much she was feeling for him
or that it was so much bigger than what she'd felt
for him when they first met.

She held him, rubbing her hands up and down
his back, wishing she could reach past the shadows inside him, wishing she could convince him
that he wasn't at fault. But all she could do was
show him. What she felt. What she saw when she
looked at him.

Drawing his head up, she kissed him, pouring everything she had into the kiss and was rewarded when he groaned and took everything she offered. Her head was spinning when he fast-walked her back to the bed, when he stretched her out and claimed her in every way possible.

Rita's mind blanked out and her body took over. Sensation flooded her. Tingles of awareness swarmed through her and curls of delicious tension settled in the pit of her stomach and spread like a wildfire. His hands, his mouth, moved over her, driving her wild, until the flames he lit enveloped them both.

She touched and stroked and kissed, wanting him to experience everything she was. Wanting him to know that he wasn't alone. That she was here. With him. Wanted him to *feel* the love she couldn't bring herself to say yet.

Oh, yes, she still loved him. Yes, she still wanted the happily-ever-after with him. But she knew instinctively that he wouldn't want to hear that now. So she kept it tucked inside and told herself that they were a matched set. Each of them locking away a piece of themselves they wanted no one else to see.

Then he entered her, and all thought fled. She focused only on what he was doing to her, making her feel. His body moved within hers and the incredible friction left her breathless and she didn't care. Breathing was overrated. She didn't need air when she had Jack.

He took her higher than she'd gone before, pushing her to reach for the completion she knew was waiting. Rita kept her gaze locked on his. She couldn't have looked away if it had meant her life. Those ice-blue eyes warmed and steamed and glowed with passion. Watching him and her own reflection in his eyes, she shattered, her body simply splintering into jagged pieces of pleasure that had her screaming his name and clutching his shoulders. And only a moment later, he surrendered to her, emptying himself into her and she held him while he fell.

Eight

"Don't start thinking anything's changed," Jack warned her the next morning.

Rita bit her lip and hid a smile. She had been expecting this. She'd known that after what they'd shared the night before Jack would try to pull back again. Pretend that last night hadn't happened. And she'd come up with a way to combat it. She wasn't going to argue. She was simply going to ignore *his* arguments.

Rita had had a long night to think about this. Naturally there hadn't been any snuggling or cuddling after their amazing bout of lovemaking—

and that's what it had been whether he admitted it or not. It wasn't just sex. It was making love. And though Rita had spent the rest of the night alone in the guest room, she'd been more hopeful than she had been in six months.

He might not realize it yet, but there was a chink in the wall he was hiding behind. For one brief moment, he'd let his guard down. Let her in. Sure, he'd slammed it shut again quickly, but now that she'd made it through once, she was determined to do it again. Alone in the silence of her own room, Rita had vowed to smash those walls around Jack until nothing was left but the two of them standing in the rubble.

"Okay," she said brightly. "Got it. Nothing's changed. This ship is just gorgeous."

"What?"

She looked at him, pleased to see the confusion on his features. If she kept him off balance, it would be harder for him to plant his feet behind that damn wall.

"I said this ship is gorgeous." Rita did a fast circle on the main deck of *The Sea Queen*, taking in the gleaming wood floors, the shining windows and the sweep of sea stretching out behind it. "I've never been on a cruise ship before. For some reason I didn't realize just how *big* they are."

"Yeah," he said irritably, "it's great."

"Thanks for inviting me along to see the ship."

"I didn't invite you. *You* invited you."

"True," she said with a shrug, "but you didn't fight me on it. That was practically gracious. Congrats."

He frowned again and Rita had to fight to hide the smile tugging at her mouth. "So, do you really have to meet with the captain?"

Still frowning, he glanced around, then up at the bridge. "Just to say hello, let him know I'm doing a walk-through."

"Do you want me with you or can I wander?"

"Come with me, then wander," he said, heading toward the wide open doors that led to the main lobby and reception area.

Rita was grinning as she followed him inside, then she stopped dead, her mouth dropped open and she did a slow turn to take it all in.

The Sea Queen was palatial. A tiled floor was inlaid with a depiction of what looked like a Middle Ages golden crown. There was a staircase that was so wide she suspected trucks could pass through side by side. Copper railings lined the second and third stories that looked down onto the lobby and deep scarlet rugs climbed the stairs. The ceiling was draped with pendant lights in shades of copper and brass and the walls boasted murals of what, again, looked like the Middle Ages. There was a theme here that went toward ancient royalty, with a hint of magic.

"At night, the pendant lights glow, and starlight flickers against the black ceiling."

"Wow." She didn't even look at him. "I seriously love this. It's very…magical. I half expect to see wizards and witches walk through the doors."

"Good," he said, shoving both hands into the pockets of his black jeans. "That's what we were going for. The club rooms and bars are all done with the same kind of decor. A little mystical. A lot upscale."

Now she did look at him in time to see a flash of pride cross his face. "It's really spectacular," she said.

Nodding, he said, "Let's find the captain, then I'll show you a few of the staterooms."

She took his hand and counted it a victory when he didn't shake her off, instead holding on to her fingers as if she were a lifeline.

On the bridge, Rita was stunned. It was a huge room, with windows giving the crew an incredibly wide view of the sea. There were enough computers to make it look like a spaceship rather than a cruise ship.

Captain McManus, a tall, gray-haired man with sharp brown eyes and an easy smile, welcomed them both then took Jack to one side to go over a few things. Rita didn't mind. It gave her a chance to look around and appreciate the nearly bird's-eye view of the ocean and the Long Beach harbor.

There were two tall command chairs that reminded her of something off the Starship *Enterprise*'s bridge and counters filled with screens, blinking lights and men and women busily going over everything. She could only imagine how busy they were when they were actually at sea.

And what would that be like, she wondered.

Being on this luxurious ship, sailing off to other countries, meeting new people. She looked up at Jack. "You've been on a lot of cruises, haven't you?"

"A few," he said, looking out over the water. "When we were kids, my folks liked to pile us all on one of the ships for a couple of weeks." His features softened at the good memory. "Mom used to say it was the only way she could get all of us to stay in the same place for any length of time."

"That must have been fun," she said, a little wistfully. "I've never been on one myself. Just a little too spooky, I guess. All of that water—"

He shook his head and said, "Doesn't seem that way, though. Once you're on board, it's like you're on your own private island."

"Well," she said, glancing around, "this ship is big enough that maybe even I wouldn't be nervous."

"I can't imagine you scared of anything," Jack said.

She looked up into his eyes. If he only knew that the one thing that scared her was losing him again. She'd mourned him once and now she had him back. Rita was determined that she wouldn't let him go this time.

"You ready to see other parts of the ship?"

She half turned to look up at Jack. "Sure. I'd love to. But first let me say, the bridge is amazing. And a little disappointing, too," she added.

"Really?" The captain laughed and asked, "Why?"

"Well, it sounds silly, but I sort of expected to see a wheel up here."

Jack smiled and the captain let out a laugh that had several of his officers turning to stare at him in surprise.

"No," Captain McManus said finally. "Everything's done by computer now. Not as romantic but much more efficient."

"I suppose," she said, then held out one hand to the man. "Thank you for letting me look around."

"For the boss's wife?" He shook her hand and winked. "Anytime at all."

"Thanks, Captain," Jack said. "We'll let you get back to it."

"Excellent. We'll be ready to sail on time, Mr. Buchanan."

"Good to know."

When they left, Rita took Jack's hand again and walked beside him on the catwalk surrounding the bridge. The sea air flew fast and furious this high up and gave her a chill that was dispelled by Jack's big hand holding hers.

"We'll take the elevator down and I'll show you the theatres, the pools and a few of the club and casino lounges."

"Okay." She whipped her hair back to look up at him. "So, you're glad you invited me along?"

His lips twitched. "I didn't invite you."

"You wish you had."

"Maybe." He glanced at her, gave her hand a squeeze, then steered her into an elevator.

There were mirrors on every surface and Rita couldn't help but look at him. The man was so gorgeous, she could have stared at him for hours. His features were strong and sharp and had been honed down over the last several months, giving him the look of a saint with a wicked side.

He met her gaze in the mirror and just for a second, the power of his stare was enough to punch her heart into a frantic beat.

"You okay?"

"Fine," she said, though she really wasn't. How could she be, when she was in love with a man who didn't want to be loved?

The elevator stopped with a ding and he announced, "First stop, Deck Three."

Just like the rest of the ship, it was elegant and luxurious, from the brass sconces on the walls to the dark ruby carpet on the floor. Then her gaze focused on the solid white surface stretching out in front of them. "There's an ice-skating rink?"

He laughed. "We've got everything."

Her imagination completed the picture, with families moving across the ice, laughing, making memories. She could almost hear them echoing in the now-empty space.

"Oh, I miss skating," she said, and rubbed one hand over her belly. "But my center of gravity's a little whacked right now, so…"

"Yeah, well, you can always skate when you're back in Utah after the baby's born."

It was a slap. A reminder. *Don't get comfortable*, he was saying. *I won't let you in. I won't let you stay. I won't let myself care.*

Rita almost swayed with the emotional impact, but she locked her knees because she couldn't let him see what he could so easily do to her. She wanted to argue with him, tell him she loved him and she wasn't going anywhere. But Rita remembered that she'd made the decision to simply not engage when he pulled back. When he tried to shut her out. So she smiled instead, though that small curve of her mouth cost her more than he would ever know.

"Yes. There's plenty of time for skating after the baby." She looked around. "Where's the theatre? What movie's playing?"

"Not a movie theatre," he said, frowning at her, as if waiting for her real reaction to what he'd said. "It's for live shows. The movies are up on Deck Eight, along with a spa and a casino and stuff for the kids and—" He broke off. "Hell, who can remember it all?"

"So, show me." She started walking in the direction he'd pointed. He was still holding her hand though and tugged her to a stop.

"Rita, last night, what I told you—"

"It's okay, Jack. Whatever you tell me is safe with me," she assured him.

"It's not that. It's…" He paused, took a breath and then released it again. "I want you to know that I made a vow to myself. You keep telling me how I'm keeping my family—and you—at a distance. You're right. But it's with a purpose. I swore I would never put anyone in the position of mourning me—and now I've got you. And the baby. And if I let my family get close again, let *you* get close, then I risk causing pain. I won't do it."

She didn't even know what to say to that.

"Rita—" His eyes were shadowed. "Bottom line, I don't want to hurt you."

Foolish man. Couldn't he see that's exactly what he was doing? Did he really believe that causing pain *now* was better than later? His family was already in pain because they couldn't reach him. And she knew just how they felt. But Rita knew he wouldn't want to hear that.

"Good." She nodded sharply. "I don't want to hurt you, either."

"Great. But my point is…"

"Oh, don't worry so much, Jack." She looked at him and the sunlight filtering through all the windows threw golden light across his face. "I get it. Nothing's changed. You're still locking yourself away from the world to save the rest of us."

He didn't want to hurt her, but he didn't want to love her, either. She had to force a smile again and he would never know how much it cost her.

He frowned. "That's—"

Rita kept her voice light, as she added, "Not important right now. I said I don't want to hurt you, but I might if you don't show me where the closest bathroom is. Honestly, this baby must be camped out on my bladder."

"Oh. Right." With the subject neatly changed,

he led her down one side of the ship and waited as she went inside.

Rita hadn't really needed the bathroom, for a change. What she'd needed was a minute or two to herself. To think. To search her heart and find the strength to keep pretending that he couldn't rip a chunk out of her soul with a word.

She gripped the edge of the black marble countertop and stared into the mirror at her own reflection. Her eyes had so many things to say and she didn't want to hear any of them. Maybe she was being foolish for loving a man who so clearly wasn't interested in making the same kind of commitment.

But how could she simply stop?

Besides, the very fact that he was trying to warn her off, save her from him, told her that he *did* care. More than he wanted to.

"And, it's not like you get a *choice* about who you love," she told her reflection. And scowled a little when her mirror image mocked her. "Fine," she admitted, "even if I *had* a choice, I'd still choose him."

Did that make her a martyr? An idiot? "Neither," she decided, staring into her own eyes. "It makes me Rita Marchetti Buchanan. I love him. It's as simple as that, really."

Nodding to herself, she shook her hair back, gave her baby belly a consoling rub, then lifted her chin and went back to face her husband with a smile.

The next few days weren't easy. Jack had expected Rita to be a little more...depressed, he guessed, about the fact that he'd brushed off their night of sex as changing nothing.

Of course, it *had*, he just couldn't admit that. Not to himself and certainly not to her. But the truth was, now that he'd been with her again, that was all he could think about.

Apparently, though, Rita was having a much easier time of it. She'd moved on as if she'd felt nothing and that he knew was a damn lie. He'd watched her, heard her, *felt* her response to their lovemaking. But she'd set it all aside and rather than being relieved, Jack was just a little ticked off. What the hell?

She wasn't talking about it and he'd fully expected her to go all female on him. Women always wanted to *talk*. To *share*. The fact that Rita wasn't bugged him. He couldn't put his finger on what was happening and that bothered him, too. Jack felt off balance somehow and he wasn't sure when that had happened.

His new reality was simply marching on as if nothing had changed at all. Every morning, since he refused to have her drive across town all by herself at four thirty in the morning, he was up and taking her to the bakery. Where she made him coffee and fresh pastries and they had breakfast together while she talked nonstop, telling him stories about her family, talking about her plans for the bakery, refusing to accept his silence.

She pushed him for his opinion and when she didn't agree with him, she goaded him into an argument. Hell, he hadn't talked this much in the four months since he'd been home.

Every night, she was right there, whether she

was cooking in the penthouse kitchen or they were ordering takeout. Rita made him a part of it. She poked and prodded at him until she got him to talk about his work, about their tour of *The Sea Queen*, readying to set sail. She poked her nose into his relationship with his brother, sister and father. Nothing was sacred, Jack told himself. The woman was making herself such a presence in his life, he couldn't ignore her in spite of how hard he tried.

And every night, when she was in the guest room and he was alone in his huge, empty bed, he really tried. But her face was uppermost in his mind all the damn time. He closed his eyes to sleep and she was there. The pillow she'd used still carried her scent.

How the hell was a man supposed to do the right thing when everything in him was demanding he do the *wrong* thing?

"Hey, Jack?"

He closed his eyes and sighed a little. Even shutting himself up in his home office the minute he got home didn't work. Rita would not be stopped. "What is it?"

"Someone's here to see you."

What was she up to now? he wondered. Had she brought his whole family over? Hers? Were they all going to sit in a circle and hold hands? Frowning, he pushed up from the desk, crossed the room and stalked out into the living room, half-ready for battle.

Rita was sitting on the couch, smiling at the man opposite her. Jack stopped dead when he spotted the man's wheelchair. *Kevin.* Had to be. His chest felt tight as if something was squeezing his lungs like a lemon trying for as much juice as possible. His gaze snapped to Rita. Had she done this? No. Of course not. He hadn't even told her Kevin's last name. There was no way she could have found him and arranged to get him to the penthouse.

So what the hell was going on?

"There he is!" Rita shot him a wide, bright smile of welcome. "Jack, look who's here."

The guy in the chair turned to face him and suddenly, time did a weird shift and it was nearly five months ago. The sun felt hot, oppressive. Screams tore at the air and Kevin's curses were loud and inventive as Jack worked to stop the bleeding. He felt again the raw desperation and the sense of helplessness as he shouted for a medic.

He was standing in the penthouse and yet he had one foot firmly planted in the past and no idea how to escape it.

"Dude," Kevin said on a laugh. "You look like you just saw a ghost."

In a way, he had, Jack told himself and shook his head, trying to clear the images rising up in his mind. For just a second, he'd seen Kevin as he'd been before that last mission. Tall, strong, laughing. Now reality was back and he didn't know what to say. "Surprised to see you is all."

"Yeah. It's been a while." Kevin rested his forearms on the arms of his chair and folded his hands together. His blond hair was just a little longer than it had been in the corps and his blue eyes were sharp, shrewd and locked on Jack. He'd lost some weight, but the real difference was the pinned-up legs of the slacks he wore.

Kevin Davis had lost both legs on that mission, in spite of the medics delivering fast, heroic care. And Jack hadn't talked to him since the morning he'd been evacced to a hospital ship. Even then, it had been less of a conversation and more of Kevin damning Jack to hell for saving him. Not something he liked to think about.

"You gonna say hello anytime soon?" Kevin asked with a tilted grin.

"Yeah. Sure." Jack crossed the room, held out one hand and looked down at his friend. "Good to see you, Kev."

After shaking hands, Jack sat on the couch beside Rita and asked, "So what brings you here?"

"Cut right to the chase, no bull," Kevin said, smiling even wider. "Haven't changed much, Sarge."

For a second, Jack felt a twinge. He'd been in the military for so long that becoming a civilian again had been a stretch. Now he wasn't sure where the hell he belonged. Then he felt Rita's hand sneak into his and though he told himself not to accept the comfort she was offering, his fingers linked through hers and locked them together.

Guilt pinged around the center of his chest like a Ping-Pong ball on steroids. Here he sat. Beautiful, pregnant wife. Elegant penthouse. Successful business. His life hadn't been shattered. He'd simply stepped back into it and though it hadn't been an easy adjustment, it had been nothing compared to what Kevin had no doubt gone through. Jack's tours of duty hadn't cost him what they had Kevin. And he couldn't make himself be okay with that.

His back teeth ground together and he fought against the rising tide of regret within. This was why he hadn't answered Kevin's email. Hell, why he hadn't even opened it. His memories were thick and rich enough that he didn't need a reminder—being with Kevin in person—to make them even more so. And hell, what could he say to the man? Kevin had lost his legs. Jack had come home whole, if changed. How was that fair?

How could he look into the man's eyes, knowing that it was he who had been leading that squad? It was Jack's decisions that had eventually brought about what had happened to Kevin. If they'd zigged instead of zagged, what might have changed? A man could drive himself crazy with thoughts like that.

How could Kevin not still blame him?

Jack had spent months trying to get past the memories of that one fateful day and hadn't been able to do it. How much more difficult was it for Kevin to try to move past it when every day he was faced with a physical reminder of his own limitations?

"Jack," Kevin said quietly, as if he knew exactly what his friend was thinking, feeling, *remembering*. "You don't have to do this. Don't have to feel bad for me. I'm fine. Really."

Now, looking into his old friend's eyes, Jack couldn't find any blame there, any anger. And that alone surprised him enough that he couldn't get his head straight.

Jack felt Rita give his hand a squeeze and he appreciated it. "I can see that. I'm glad for it."

"Now all you have to do is accept it." His friend nodded, kept his eyes fixed on Jack's. "Took me a long time, I admit it. For weeks after it happened, I'd wake up and try to swing my legs out of bed." A rueful smile curved his mouth. "Could have sworn I felt them there."

"Kevin—"

"I didn't come here to make things harder for you, Jack."

"Why are you here, then?" He managed to get the question out even though he was worried about the answer.

"To see you, you damn fool," Kevin said, leaning back in his chair, shaking his head. "You never answered the email I sent you two months ago. Hell, you never even opened it."

"Yeah." Jack nodded. "Sorry about that. I just—"

"I get it," Kevin said. "You still should have read it, though. Would have saved me a drive up from San Diego."

Jack smiled at that. He and Kevin had formed a friendship at first because they were both from Southern California. Just a couple hours away from each other by freeway, so they'd had a lot of the same experiences. They'd formed a tighter bond, of course, as all military in combat did, but it had begun on the California connection.

"So," Kevin was saying, waving one hand at the chair and his missing legs, "a lot of things have changed. Obviously."

Jack watched his friend, looking for some sign of anger or bitterness or blame and couldn't find any. Instead, he looked…comfortable in his skin. In that chair.

"But, hey," Kevin added, smiling at Rita. "Looks like you've had some pretty big changes, too. You're married now, having a baby."

Jack glanced at Rita, and when she smiled at him, he felt that tug of guilt again. Kevin couldn't know that this was a temporary arrangement. And there was no way Jack would let him know. He forced himself to look back to Kevin. "I'm glad you're okay."

"I'm better than okay." Kevin shook his head and gave Jack a wry smile. "If you'd bothered to open the damn email I sent you like two months ago, you would have known that."

Jack ran his free hand across his jaw. "I know. I'm sorry. I should have. I just didn't want to go over what happened again."

"Hey," Kevin said softly, "neither do I. Look, Jack, last time I saw you, things were a little… *tense*."

Jack laughed shortly and held on a little more tightly to Rita's hand. "You could say that."

"Why don't I go make some coffee?" Rita looked at both men. "I'll give you guys some time to talk."

"Not necessary," Kevin told her. "I can't stay long, anyway, so don't go to any trouble for me."

"Stay, Rita," Jack said, looking into her eyes. He wanted her there. It surprised him to acknowledge just how much he wanted her beside him. Seeing Kevin again, watching him maneuver that wheelchair, tore at Jack and damned if he didn't want the connection to Rita to help him get through it.

When the hell had *that* happened? When had he started counting on her?

"If you're worried I'm here to cuss you out again for saving my butt, don't be." Kevin moved the chair in closer and linked his gaze to Jack's. "I remember it all, you know?"

"Yeah. I know." So did he. Every damn night, he remembered it. He always would.

Kevin smiled, nodded. "'Course you do. Hard to forget something like that—you doing your best to save me while I'm telling you to shoot me."

"Kevin—"

"Nah, man," he said, holding up one hand to keep Jack quiet. "I'm not here to go over it all again." He grinned. "Once was enough, trust me. I just wanted to say *thank you*."

"What?" Confused now, Jack just stared at him.

"Well, that surprised you," Kevin said wryly. "Yeah. Thank you. Thanks for saving me even when I was too stupid to want to be saved." He blew out a breath, dragged his fingers through his hair. "I swear, being furious at you got me through those first few days."

Jack nodded, took a breath and held it.

"But one day I realized that I like breathing," Kevin said. "So I started being less mad at you."

"Glad to hear it."

Kevin shrugged. "I'm not saying it was easy, getting used to being shorter—"

Rita smiled and he winked at her.

"But I did. And I'm here to tell you, alive is better than dead." Kevin held his hand out to Jack. "So thanks, man. Thanks for—hell. For everything."

Jack took his hand and felt one or two of those straws of guilt fall from his shoulders. He still had plenty left of course, but there was a sigh of relief to know that at least some of the burden had been eased. And Kevin *did* look good. Yeah, he was in a chair, but he looked strong and well and, damn it, *happy*. Jack had worried about his friend, thought that maybe he'd never really find any kind of contentment again.

"You're really okay."

"I'm *better* than okay, dude." Kevin slapped Jack's shoulder. "Again, man. Read your emails."

Rita squeezed Jack's hand again and in spite of the easing of the tension within, he held on to her tightly. "So why don't you just tell me what's in the email?"

"Turns out you're not the only one settling down. I'm getting married, can you believe it?" Kevin laughed, shook his head and said, "Lisa's a nurse. Hell, she was *my* nurse at Walter Reed. I showed up there all full of myself and complaining and she just would not listen." Still smiling, he continued, "The woman refused to let me bitch. She ignored my crappy moods and pushed me to come back to life when I really didn't want to."

Well, hell. Jack felt Rita's hand in his and told himself that he and Kevin had a lot more in common than he would have guessed. Wasn't that just what Rita had been doing to *him* for the last few weeks? Prodding, pushing, refusing to give up and go away.

"Anyway, Lisa's a California girl—her folks

live in Oceanside—weird, huh? Go halfway around the world to meet a girl who lived about twenty minutes from me?" Kevin laughed a little. "So I got along so well, they transferred me to a hospital out here and Lisa made the move, too. We're getting married at my folks' place."

"Congratulations," Rita said, giving Jack a nudge.

"Right, yeah. I'm happy for you, man."

"Hey, there's more. We're having a baby, too."

Surprised again, Jack blurted, "Really?"

"Hey, man," Kevin said, grinning, "I didn't lose any of the important bits over there in that hell-hole."

Rita laughed and Jack just shook his head. "Damn, Kev. You really haven't changed much, have you?"

"Older, wiser, shorter," Kevin said, then his smile slowly faded away. "Look, I had to make this drive to see you in person because my wedding is this weekend."

"So soon?"

Kevin's eyebrows lifted. "When I emailed you, I gave you two months' warning."

"Right." Jack nodded. "My fault."

"Absolutely true," Kevin agreed easily. "But the point is, I drove my ass all the way up here to ask you to be my best man."

"Your—" Okay, Jack didn't know how many more surprises he could take. He never would have expected the man he'd believed hated his guts to ask him to stand up for him.

"Best man. Yeah. Because that's what you are." His features sober, serious, Kevin said, "We were buds before. Been through a lot of crap together. But what you did for me, Jack, I can never repay."

A twist of pain wrung at his heart. "You don't have to."

"Yeah, I know that. Doesn't stop the need." Kevin glanced at Rita. "Your man was always a stand-up. He kept me alive in a place that tried its best to kill me."

Rita reached out instinctively and took his hand with her free hand, somehow linking the two men even more completely than they already were.

Kevin released her hand, and reached into the pocket of his black leather jacket. He drew out a cream-colored envelope that he handed to Rita.

"I'm giving this to you for two reasons," he said. "One, you're way better looking than Jack."

"You're a very astute man," Rita said, grinning. Beside her, Jack only sighed.

"And two, more important, you'll make sure he gets to the wedding. Right?" He looked at her meaningfully for a long moment.

Then Rita leaned forward, kissed Kevin's cheek and said, "You bet I will." She glanced back at Jack as if for confirmation. "We'll be there. Won't we?"

"Yeah." He looked from Rita to Kevin and back again. "We'll be there, Kev."

"Good." He clapped his hands together then scrubbed his palms. "Then my work here is done and my lovely bride-to-be is going to be picking me up outside in—" He checked his watch. "Ten minutes. We're going for dinner, then taking the long drive home."

"Do you really have to go so soon?" Rita asked,

standing up as Kevin wheeled back and turned. "Why don't both of you come up and have dinner with us?"

"No, but thanks." Kevin looked knowingly at Jack. "I think we're both going to need a little time to get used to the new us, right, Jack?"

It would take time and it was good to know that Kevin not only understood but felt the same. Too many emotions were churning inside him. Waves were rocking his insides like a storm at sea and he had a lot of thinking to do. "Yeah. A little time would be a good thing."

Kevin nodded solemnly, but his gaze locked with Jack's. "We'll get there. But we'll see you Saturday?"

Just as somber, Jack promised, "I swear. We'll be there."

Nine

Once Kevin was gone, Jack gave in to the tension screaming inside him. Stalking across the room, he made for the terrace, pushing open the French doors and stepping into the icy blast of wind that rushed at him. He turned his face into that wind and wished to hell it could blow all of his churning thoughts right out of his head.

"Jack?"

Teeth gritted, he kept his gaze on the expanse of the ocean streaked with the brilliant colors of sunset rather than turn to face the woman who'd become too important to him. Until Kevin had come by tonight, Jack hadn't realized just how much he'd come to depend on Rita's presence in his life. He was already in too deep, he knew that because of just how much he'd needed her by his side when Kevin was in the house. Needed her to anchor him.

And that bothered Jack plenty.

"Are you okay?" Her voice was soft, husky, filled with concern that scraped at him. He didn't want her worried about him, caring about him, God help him, *loving* him.

He'd once vowed that he would never put anyone in the position of having to mourn him. And the more she cared, the more pain she risked. How was he supposed to stand by and let her get deeper into feelings that would only carry the promise of future pain?

Damn it, this marriage was supposed to be temporary. Supposed to be emotion-free. A bargain. Yet somehow, in spite of his best efforts it had turned into more. The question now was, what was he prepared to do about it?

"Jack?" she asked again. "Are you okay?"

"Fine." He bit the word off, hoping she'd take the damn hint for once and leave him alone. Give him enough space to get himself together again. To find the center that had slipped out of his grasp the minute he saw Kevin in that chair.

"You don't sound fine," she said and came up beside him. She shivered in the cold wind and rubbed her hands up and down her arms for warmth. She was only wearing white capris and a short-sleeved pink T-shirt. Her bare feet had to be freezing on the concrete floor. But she wasn't leaving. He knew her well enough now to expect that.

When he didn't speak, she tried another tack. "Kevin seems nice."

Nice. Yeah, he was. He was also smart. Funny. And in a damn chair for the rest of his life. Jack closed his eyes briefly. "You don't have to do this."

"What am I doing?"

"Helping." He glanced at her. "I don't need your help. And I don't need to be soothed."

"That's what you think?" she asked, leaning

against the railing to look up at him. "Everybody needs help sometimes, Jack. You're not a super-hero."

Silently, he laughed at the idea. He was as far from a superhero as anyone could get.

"Didn't say I was and if I want help," he added, shooting her a dark look that should have sent her skittering for cover, "I'll ask for it."

Naturally, he told himself, Rita paid no atten-tion to his warning look. Instead, she laughed and the raw, sexy sound awakened every cell in his body.

"Sure, you'll ask for help. Jack," she said with a smile. "You wouldn't ask for water if you were on fire."

The fact that she was right only irritated him further. How much more was he expected to take tonight? Facing down a friend whose life was forever changed wasn't enough? God, he needed time alone. He needed to *think*.

"You're staring out at that ocean like you ex-pect to find answers there."

"I don't need answers, either," he ground out.

"I just need some space. Time. Some damn solitude. God, I can't even remember what it's like to be completely alone anymore."

That insult sailed right over her head. She just didn't listen to what she didn't want to hear. In a way, he admired that about her. Even when it worked against him.

"If you think you can insult me into walking away, you're wrong."

Exasperated, he blew out a breath. "Then what will it take?"

"There's nothing you can do that will make me leave you alone right now," Rita said. "You've had enough solitude, Jack. Maybe too much."

"Fine. You won't leave, I will." He turned, but stopped when she laid one hand on his arm.

"I've got some of those answers you don't need." She paused and he knew she was waiting for him to look at her. Finally, he did.

"What are you talking about now?"

Shrugging, she said, "You said you didn't need answers, but you do. And here's one for you. You've been torturing yourself for months over

Kevin, Jack. But there was no need. You saw him. He's happy."

He scraped one hand across his face. "He's in a chair."

"That's not your fault."

"Yeah, well, saying it doesn't make that true." He shifted his gaze back out to the water and watched that darkening surface churn with the wind. Looking out at the sky and sea was so much easier than looking into whiskey-colored eyes that saw too much. "You weren't there. I was."

"So was Kevin," she pointed out, refusing to let it go. "And he doesn't blame you."

"He should." His gaze narrowed on that wide, roiling water and he felt it replicated in his own soul. "Damn it, if I had made a different call, it wouldn't have happened."

"My God, you're stubborn," she said, sliding over to stand between him and the railing, so that he was forced to look at her. "Yes, you were in charge and you made the decisions, but making different ones might not have kept everyone safe. Maybe a different call would have killed Kevin.

Or you. Or someone else. There's just no way to know and no point in continuing to drag yourself over the coals like this."

He shook his head. He couldn't speak. What was there to say, anyway? She couldn't get it and he didn't blame her. No one who wasn't there could ever understand what it was to hold men's lives in your hands. One wrong call and people died. Or lost their legs.

"Are you really so determined to carry the weight of the world?"

She made it sound as though he were being self-indulgent. Nothing could have been further from the truth. He had a right to feel like a damn bastard for what had happened to Kevin. To the new guy in their squad, DeSantos, who had *died* in that skirmish. Was he supposed to just close it off, pretend it hadn't happened? He couldn't do that. "Leave it alone, Rita."

"He thanked you for saving him, Jack."

"I was there," he pointed out, barely sparing her a glance. She didn't get it. Didn't know what it had been like to see his best friend lying wounded in front of him and not being able to do a damn thing about it. Didn't understand the guilt of coming home with both arms, both legs. Didn't know what it was to keep all of that locked inside you until you felt like you were going to explode.

This was why he'd never talked to his family. He couldn't share with them what they couldn't understand. Oh, they would try, but their pity for him would get tangled up in the facts and they'd only end up *more* worried about him than they already were.

She laid both hands on his chest and the heat of her slid inside him like a welcome balm, easing the harsh waves of regret and anger and frustration still roiling within. As much as he loved her touch, he almost resented it because it was temporary. She wouldn't be here for much longer and when she was gone it would be so much harder to be without her.

"Jack. If Kevin can move on, why can't you?"

He dropped his gaze to hers. Those whiskey eyes stared up at him with so many emotions rushing through them he couldn't begin to name them all. And it was probably better if he didn't try.

"Because," he said slowly, "if I move on, it's forgetting. And if I let myself forget, then I've learned nothing."

She tipped her head to one side and all those amazing dark brown curls fell off her shoulder to be lifted in the ever-present wind. "That makes zero sense, Jack."

One corner of his mouth lifted. Of course it didn't make sense to her. How could she untangle his emotions when they were so jumbled together even *he* didn't understand half of them. But right now, that didn't matter. She was there, pressed up against him, her curvy body radiating heat, the mound of their child between them and Jack let himself simply *feel*. If things were different, if he were different… But wishing wouldn't make it so.

She wrapped her arms around his middle and laid her head on his chest. Her scent enveloped him completely and he felt as if he were bathing in some soft, golden light. The tension she eased and soothed wasn't gone, just buried. It was all still inside him, twisting, writhing. But that didn't mean he had to find answers tonight.

He took a breath, drew her scent deep and let it ease every jagged corner of his soul. Closing his eyes, he held her close and told himself that just for tonight, he would take the comfort she offered.

And be grateful.

A couple of days later, they were in a backyard with a wildly spectacular garden bursting with blooms in every color imaginable. A rare June day of sunshine washed out of a clear blue sky and shone down like a blessing on the small group of people gathered.

The wedding was beautiful. Small, as Rita and Jack's had been, but instead of the beach, they were in a lush backyard with a small group of guests. There were tables, chairs and a wooden dance floor constructed just for the occasion. Music streamed from a stereo, an eclectic mix of classic rock, old standards and even a waltz or two just for tradition's sake.

Seated at a table in the shade, Rita looked at her husband, sitting beside her. Jack wore a perfectly tailored black suit with a white shirt and a dark blue tie. His black hair was a little long, his blue eyes a little too sharp, his jaw a little too tense. But he was there for Kevin, as promised.

Rita smoothed the skirt of her bright yellow dress across her thighs, and swung the loose fall of her hair back behind her shoulders. Reaching across their table, she took Jack's hand in hers.

"Look at them," she said, smiling. "They're so happy."

She watched Kevin, with Lisa in his lap, wheel around the dance floor. The newlyweds were laughing, kissing and completely caught up in each other. Maybe it was the pregnancy hormones, but Rita's eyes blurred with tears as she watched the two people so obviously in love.

"Yeah, they do look happy," Jack said and deliberately slid his hand out from under hers. He picked up his bottle of beer and took a long swig.

"But you don't." Sitting beside him, surrounded

by strangers in a flower-filled garden, Rita felt a now-familiar darkness creeping closer.

There didn't seem to be anything she could do to lift the cloud that had settled on him since seeing Kevin again a few days ago. He wasn't angry or even unkind. He was…civil. He treated her as he would a stranger, with a cool politeness that chipped away at her heart and soul.

When they were first married, Jack had kept a distance between them, but Rita had still sensed that he cared for her. That there was something inside him fighting to get out. Now, it was as if he'd suddenly built the wall around his heart thicker and higher, defying her to break through. God knew she'd spent the last couple of days trying to do just that. But it was as if he was on another planet—one she couldn't reach.

He slanted her a long, thoughtful look. The dappled shade from the trees threw a pattern of dark and light across his face. His features, though, were carefully blank, as if he was determined to give her no clue at all as to what he was thinking, feeling.

"No," he said finally, "I'm not happy."

God, she got an actual chill from the ice in his voice. But she had to keep trying to get to him, to touch his heart, to make him see that he wasn't alone if he didn't want to be. "Jack, what is it? What's happening?"

"This isn't the place to talk about it," he said and lifted his beer for another drink. His gaze shifted from her to Kevin and Lisa. His features were tighter, the glint in his eyes harder and Rita was more confused than ever.

She turned her head to watch the newlyweds, too, but what she saw made her smile. Made her heart lift. Kevin, in his chair, Lisa on his lap, looking down into his eyes with an expression of pure joy on her face. The two of them might have been alone in the world as the music played and a handful of dancers moved around them.

Why couldn't Jack see the happiness all around him and let himself revel in it? Why was he more determined than ever to wallow in misery? For the first time since finding him again, Rita was worried.

* * *

As it turned out, she had a right to be.

A few hours later, they were back in the penthouse. It had been a long, silent ride, with tension building between them until Rita had felt it alive and bristling in the car. Jack had given away nothing. She still had no idea what was bothering him but she was through guessing. Rita had waited as long as she could. There was no point in worrying over something when you could face it head-on and tackle it to the ground.

Dropping her taupe clutch bag onto the nearest chair, she stared at Jack's back and demanded, "Are you going to tell me what's bugging you?"

He was standing in the center of the living room, suit jacket tossed to the couch, hands stuffed into his slacks pockets. When he turned to look at her, Rita's heart actually dropped. If a man's face could be a sheet of ice, then that's what she was looking at.

His clear blue eyes glittered like shards of that ice as they locked on her. "What's bugging me? It's this." He pulled his hands free, lifted both arms as if to encompass the two of them and the apartment. "It's over, Rita. This marriage sham? It's done. Time for you to go."

All of the air in her lungs left her in a rush and seconds later Rita was light-headed. It felt as if the floor had opened up beneath her feet and simply swallowed her. Shock was too small a word for what she was feeling. Hurt was right up there, too, but temper was coming in a close third and quickly rising to the top. Forcing herself to breathe, she stared at him as she would have a stranger. "Just like that?"

"Just like that," he said and headed for the bar in the far corner of the room. Bending down, he opened the mini fridge and grabbed a bottle of beer. After opening it, he took a long drink and avoided looking at her.

Yep, temper was bubbling to the surface and Rita gave it free rein. Her family could have told Jack that when Rita was truly angry, it was best to run, but that was all right, she told herself. He'd find that out for himself.

"That's just not going to fly with me, Jack."

One of his eyebrows lifted in mild surprise. She could do better.

"You don't get to stand there so cool and dismissive and say 'time for you to go, Rita,' and expect me to start packing," she said, riding a cresting wave of what felt like pure fury. "You don't tell me to go and then not even bother to look at me."

He slid his gaze to hers and it was almost worse, she thought, seeing the blank emptiness in his eyes. Pain grabbed at her, but she shook it off.

"What the hell happened?" she demanded. "You've been different ever since Kevin came here. And today—" she broke off, shook her head and said, "the wedding was beautiful, but you couldn't see it. Kevin and Lisa were practically glowing and you sat there like a black hole, sucking in every bit of joy around you without it once affecting you. Where's this all coming from?"

"From Kevin," he snapped, then took a breath to visibly calm himself. When he had, he continued. "From the wedding and Kevin and Lisa and the damn hearts and flowers practically floating over their heads."

She just blinked at him. This was making no sense at all. "That's a bad thing? How does your friend's happiness equate to you being miserable?"

"I'm not miserable. I'm realistic."

"It's realistic to hate the fact that people are happy? To send me away so there's no chance of *you* being happy?"

"That's right."

God, it was like talking to a wall. Only she'd probably have gotten more out of a wall. He was bulletproof. Her words bounced off him and never left a dent.

"You don't want to be happy, is that it?" God, she was getting colder.

"You're damn right," he said, setting the beer down in a deliberately calm manner. Coming out from behind the bar, he walked toward her and stopped with a good three feet of empty space between them. "I told you going in that this was temporary, just until the baby was born."

She put both hands on her belly. "News flash. Still about two months to go."

He didn't even look at the baby. Hell, he barely looked at *her*. "Yeah, but we don't have to be living together to be married, do we?" he asked.

"Wow." She took a step toward him and he took one back. One short, sharp laugh shot from her throat. "Was I getting too close, Jack? Were you starting to care? Are you making me leave because you don't want me to go?"

"Think you've got me all figured out, do you?"

"Oh, yeah," she said, nodding. "It wasn't that hard. Answer me this. Do I scare you, Jack?"

He gritted his teeth, huffed out a breath and said flatly, "You terrify me."

Small comfort, she thought, but didn't speak again as he continued.

"I didn't sign up for this. Didn't *want* this," he muttered darkly, pushing one hand through his hair impatiently. "You're getting too close, Rita. I can see it. You're starting to believe this is all *real* and it's not. It can't be. I won't let it be."

She'd never been dismissed so completely, so

casually and it hurt so much she wanted to keen, but damned if she'd let him see that. Her heart ached for them both. She'd gotten to him, reached him and because she had, he was cutting her out of his life with a single, cold stroke.

"*You* won't let it be real?" she asked. "You're the only one with a vote here?"

"That's right." His eyes were cold, empty and that one fact tore at her so deeply, Rita could hardly breathe.

"Why?" She stared at him, completely confused and hurt and even her temper was easing off to be replaced by an ache that settled around her heart and throbbed with every beat. "You at least owe me an explanation, Jack. How did Kevin showing up here and his happiness today make you so determined to throw your own chance at it away? *Our* chance."

"You want an explanation, fine. Sure, Kevin and Lisa are happy today," Jack ground out. "But what about tomorrow? What about when pain comes rolling down the track and hits them both?"

Flabbergasted, Rita stared at him. "*What?*

Being happy isn't worth it because one day you might not be? What kind of logic is that?"

He shook his head grimly. "Perfect, that's what kind. I saw it happen. Too many damn times. You love someone—or worse yet, let someone love you—and things go wrong, lives are shattered. I heard a guy's widow sobbing. I watched parents grieving." He wasn't cool and detached now. His voice was hot, words tumbling over each other. "I saw the strongest men I've ever known break under the agony of loss. Why the hell would anyone risk that? No, Rita. There's no way I'm setting either one of us up for that."

Her own breath came short and fast, because she knew he believed what he was saying. None of it made sense but that didn't keep him from having faith in every word. "So screw ever smiling or being joyful because of what *might* happen."

He didn't even flinch.

"It will happen," he insisted. "You think anybody gets through life unscathed? They don't.

The best you can do is protect yourself from misery."

"By *being* miserable?" she demanded.

"Think what you like." Shaking his head, he ignored that and said, "I'm not letting you get any deeper into this marriage, Rita." His voice was tight, hard. "You're getting too damn close, pulling me along with you, and I can't go any further. I won't let myself start coming back to life only to risk more grief. Trust me, it's not worth it. I *know*."

God, he'd already cut her off. He'd made that call a couple of days ago when Kevin visited and since then it had been solidifying in his mind until now; it was a done deal. Without talking to her about any of it, he'd made the decision to end what was between them.

"You're wrong," she whispered, and to her fury, felt tears fill her eyes. She *hated* that. Rita always ended up crying when she was at her angriest. Too much emotion had to eventually spill from her eyes and the tears were lowering. Viciously, she swiped at her eyes. "You're so wrong it's sad,

Jack. Caring about people? That's worth *everything*."

"Don't cry." He scrubbed one hand across the back of his neck. "Just don't. It'll rip at me because I...*care* about you."

"You don't just care, Jack," she told him flatly. "You love me."

His gaze snapped to hers. "See? That's another reason you have to leave."

"What?"

"Love's coming, and I know that, too. So I need you gone before I love you."

Rita laughed shortly then actually reached up and tugged at her hair in frustration. This had to be the weirdest and most heartbreaking conversation she'd ever had. "Right. Don't want to take a chance on actually *loving* someone."

"I'm doing what I have to do."

"No, you're not, Jack," she said, lifting her chin and meeting that cold stare with all the heat she could muster. "You're doing what's easiest."

"You think this is *easy*?" he demanded.

"I think it's unnecessary," she snapped. "But no

worries. I'm leaving. I'll be out of here tonight."
Damned if she'd stay with a man who was so determined not to love her. To cut himself off from any feeling at all.

"You don't have to go tonight," he said. "Tomorrow's soon enough."

Her gaze locked on his. "No, it's really not."

A couple of hours later, Jack was alone in the apartment.

As good as her word, Rita was gone so fast, she'd been nothing but a blur. She hadn't said another word to him, but her silence came across loud and clear. He hadn't wanted to hurt her and someday soon, Rita would realize that he'd done all of this to protect her. He didn't want her hurt. Mourning him as he'd seen others mourn the fallen.

She'd cried.

He slapped one hand to the center of his chest in a futile attempt to ease the ache centered there. Jack had never seen Rita cry before. Not even the day he'd left her in that hotel to go back to his tour of duty. She'd sent him off with a smile that had no doubt cost her. But today, she'd cried.

If he could have changed it, he would have. But this was the only way and Jack knew it. He stepped out onto the terrace and let that cold wind slap at him. He finally had what he'd wanted—*craved*—most. Solitude. There was no one here talking to him, trying to make him laugh, drawing him back into a world he'd deliberately turned his back on.

"This is for the best. For both of us. Hell," he added, thinking of the baby, "for all three of us."

Didn't feel like it at the moment, but he was sure it would. One day. Rita would see it, too. Eventually.

"Damn it," he said when the doorbell rang. He thought about not answering it, but even as he considered it, the damn thing rang again.

"Rita probably forgot something," he told himself as he headed back inside. He took a peek through the judas hole and sighed heavily. So much for solitude.

Reluctantly, he opened the door and said, "Hi, Cass."

"Don't you 'hi' me," his sister said as she pushed past him into the apartment. She threw her purse onto the couch, then turned around, hands at her hips and glared at him. "What the hell is wrong with you?"

Calmly, Jack closed the door and faced his sister. She was practically vibrating with anger. Her eyes, so much like his own, were flashing dangerously and her features were set like stone in an expression of indignation. "What're you talking about?"

"Rita called me from the airport."

That threw him. "The *airport*?"

"Yeah, she found a flight to Utah and she went back to see her family."

Okay, he'd wanted her to leave the apartment—not the state. He wasn't sure how he felt about her being so far away. Was she planning on staying there? Giving up her bakery? Her friends?

"Are you out of your mind for real?" she asked.

"This is none of your business, Cass."

"Since we're family, it *is* my business," she countered grimly. "Rita asked me to come and check on you," Cass added, not bothering to hide the disgust in her tone. "She was worried about *you*."

"Which is just one of the reasons I asked her to go," Jack said calmly. "I don't want her worrying about me."

She jerked her head back and gave him a look of pure astonishment. "Y'know," she said, "that's what people on Earth do. We worry for the people we care about."

"I don't *want* her to care about me, that's the whole point."

"Right." Cass nodded sharply, paced a little frantically for a few minutes, then came to a stop and glared at him again. "And it's all about what you want, isn't it, Jack?"

"I didn't say that."

"Oh, please," his sister countered, waving one hand at him in dismissal. "You've been saying it in every way but words for *months*."

"I'm not doing this with you, Cass," he said. "Not going to talk about it."

"Good. Because I don't care what you have to say. Not anymore. All you have to do is listen." She came closer and he saw sparks dazzling her eyes. "I've tried to be patient with you. I'm a doctor, Jack. I know what's going on with you."

"I don't need a damn doctor and if I did," he told her hotly, "I wouldn't go to my little sister."

Damned if he needed *everyone* telling him what he should do and when he should do it. And he *really* didn't want his younger sister standing there like the voice of God telling him to shape up.

"Yes, you've made that abundantly clear and I've really tried to keep quiet, give you room to deal."

"There's nothing going on with me."

"You denying PTSD doesn't make it go away. My God, you're practically a textbook case." She walked to the couch, dropped onto it, then just as quickly jumped to her feet again, apparently unable to sit still. "I told Sam and Dad they had to give you time. Let you get used to being back in the world. That you'd come around eventually."

"I'm fine," he insisted but saw that his sister wasn't buying it.

"Sure you are." She snorted. "You notice Sam doesn't come up from San Diego much anymore? Or have you paid any attention to the fact that Dad almost never comes into the office these days even though he used to love it?"

He thought about that for a minute or two. She had a point though he'd never really considered it before. His brother, Sam, was a busy guy. And his father had recently taken up golf, so why would he be coming around an office he'd retired from. "Yeah, but—"

"Sam got tired of you shooting him down every time he tried to spend time with you."

"I didn't—"

"Yeah, you did. You've shot me down often enough for me to know that and I can tell you it's no fun having a proverbial door slammed in your face every time you try to talk to someone." She took a long breath. "Damn it, Jack, we're your *family* and we deserve better."

"I just needed—"

But she kept talking. "Dad gets his heart broken just a little more whenever he's with you and can't reach you, so he stays away."

Guilt dropped onto his shoulders, but he was so used to the burden he hardly noticed. Remembering the last time he'd seen his father, Jack could admit to the sorrow he'd seen in the older man's eyes. And still… "He doesn't—"

"Not finished," she snapped. "Honestly, Jack, you make me so furious. Do you know how many men and women come home from dangerous duties and have *no one* to talk to? To count on? Do you know how lucky you are to have people who love you? Who are willing to put up with your bullshit?"

"I—"

"Does it look like I'm done?" She inhaled sharply, blew the air out in a huff and stared up at him. "You're my brother and I love you. You're Rita's husband and *she* loves you."

There was that pang around his heart again. He rubbed the spot idly, almost unconsciously. She loved him. He'd been pretty sure she did, but *knowing* it was something else again. He swallowed hard against that pounding ache in his heart and told himself that even if she did love him, he'd done the right thing.

"You don't get it, Cass." He sighed. "I don't want to be loved. Whoever loves me is just setting themselves up for a letdown later. Why do that to anybody?"

"Well, good God," Cass said, clearly stunned. "It's worse than I thought. It's not just your memories haunting you that's kept you tucked away up here in your fortress of solitude. It's something else. You're an idiot." Shaking her head, she said, "I'm so glad Mom can't see you like this, although she'd probably have kicked you into shape by now. You don't want to be loved? You don't want to feel anything for anyone? Too damn bad. Boo the hell hoo."

"What?" A choked off, surprised laugh shot from his throat. It seemed he was destined to have the women in his life constantly surprising him.

"You have a chance at something amazing, Jack, and you're letting it get away. You told the woman who loves you, the mother of your *child*," she added with emphasis, "to leave because you're scared to be hurt again. To know pain again."

"Careful, Cass," he said, voice soft. Even for his sister, he was only willing to put up with so much. He was doing the hard thing here. Why could no one see it, appreciate what it cost him?

"No, I'm done being careful. I should never have given you time to adjust, Jack," she said sadly. "That was my mistake. I should have done just what Rita did, grab hold and drag you, kicking and screaming back into life."

"It wouldn't have worked."

"We'll never know, will we?" she asked. Still shaking her head, she walked over, picked up her purse and slung it over her shoulder. "Look around Jack," she said. "You got what you wanted. You're alone. I hope you enjoy it. Because if you keep acting like a jackass—this is all you'll ever have."

He watched her go and the slam of the door behind her echoed in the stillness.

Ten

The Marchetti bakery on historic 25th Street in Ogden was in an antique brick building with sloping wood floors that creaked musically with every step. On one side of the shop was a hand-made-chocolate shop and on the other, an artisan boutique that sold local artists' work.

The bakery drew customers from all over northern Utah, so they were constantly busy, which meant the entire family—except for the younger kids—were there when Rita arrived. Her mom and sister were in the kitchen while her father and brothers ran the front of the shop and handled any deliveries. This didn't change, she thought with a smile as she glanced around at the shining display cases and the customers wandering, looking, sitting at tables and sipping lattes.

Just walking into the bakery soothed the ball of ice in the pit of her stomach. It had been the longest hour-and-a-half flight of her life to make it here from Long Beach. She hadn't told the family she was coming; there hadn't been time. She'd simply packed her things, told Casey to close up the bakery for a few days and then raced to the airport. All Rita had been able to think of was getting here, where she knew her heart was safe.

The long drive from the Salt Lake City airport had given her more time to think and she still had no answers. Hadn't she done everything she could to reach Jack? Hadn't she given him every reason to come out of the darkness? To live again?

Tears were close so she blinked furiously to keep them at bay and smiled at a woman she knew who was busily wiping chocolate off her child's mouth. Here was safety. Love. Understanding.

The joy on her father's face when he spotted her was like pouring oil on the churning waters inside her. Rita's brothers, Anthony and Marco, called out to her as she threaded her way through the crowd toward the kitchen to find her mom. Of course she had to stop along the way to say hello to people she knew and try to make small talk, while inside she was screaming.

Behind the counter, Rita was hugged hard by her dad, then passed from brother to brother before they released her.

"This is a nice surprise," her father said, then took a closer look at her face and frowned. "It *is* nice, isn't it?"

Nick Marchetti was in his sixties, with graying black hair, sharp brown eyes and a belly that was a little fuller than it used to be. Both of his sons were several inches taller than him, but it didn't matter because Nick was, just as he always had been, a force to be reckoned with.

"It's good to see you, Daddy," Rita whispered, relaxing into his familiar hug.

He kissed her cheek and said, "Go on now, go

sit down and talk to your mother. She'll be happy you're here."

"Okay." Rita nodded, slipped through the swinging door and never saw the worried frowns on the faces of the men in her family.

Stepping into the kitchen with the familiar scents and the heat from the ovens was like walking into the comfort of her childhood. Growing up, she and her siblings had spent most of their free time working in the bakery, so the memories were thick and reassuring.

Rita had gone home to Ogden hoping for a little peace and quiet and maybe some understanding. A half hour later, she told herself she'd clearly come to the wrong place for that.

"I can't believe you left," her mother said hotly. Teresa Marchetti had short black hair, carefully touched up to hide the gray every five weeks. She was a tiny woman but ruled her family like a four-star general.

Rita took a sip of the herbal tea she wasn't interested in. "Jack didn't want me there. He told me to leave."

"And so you do it?" Teresa shook her head and scowled. "I don't remember you being so obedient as a child."

Rita stiffened at the accusation. "I wasn't being obedient." God, that made her sound like some subservient fifties' housewife asking her husband for an allowance.

"Yet here you are." Her mother huffed a little, muttered something Rita didn't quite catch, then slid two trays of bread loaves into the oven. Turning back around, she reached for a bottle of water and took a drink.

It was hot in the kitchen with four ovens going constantly. Rita's father and brothers had deliberately stayed out front, leaving her mother and sister to do the heavy emotional lifting.

Gina looked up from the counter where she was rolling out cookie dough. "So Jack says go and you say okeydoke? What the hell is that, Rita?"

"Language," their mother said automatically, then added, "your sister has a point. Do you love this man?"

"Of course she does it's all over her face," Gina said before Rita could open her mouth.

"Thanks, I can talk for myself," Rita said.

"Just not to Jack, is that it?" Gina rolled her eyes as fiercely as she rolled the dough.

"I did talk to Jack." Rita broke a cookie in half and popped it into her mouth. She should have known that no one in her family would pat her on the head and simply accept what she said. They all had opinions and loved nothing better than sharing them. "I talked till my throat was dry. He doesn't listen to what he doesn't want to hear."

"Hmm," Teresa mused with a snort of amusement. "Sounds like someone else I know."

Fine, she was stubborn. Rita knew that. But this wasn't about *her*, was it?

"Mom, how could I stay if he didn't want me?"

"Oh, for God's sake," Gina blurted. "He does want you. You told us already he admitted that."

"Yes, but he doesn't *want* to want me."

"That's female logic," Anthony said when he hustled in to restock a tray of cannoli.

"Jack's the one who said it," Rita pointed out, finishing off the rest of her cookie.

Anthony countered, "He only said it because that's how men think women think."

"What?" Gina asked, clearly as confused as Rita. "That must be more male logic because it makes *no* sense."

"It does to men," Anthony argued before picking up the tray to head out front.

Rita propped her elbows on the counter and propped her head in her hands. A circus, she thought. It was a circus at Marchetti's.

"Go on, back to work," Teresa ordered, waving at her son to hurry him along. When it was just the three women in the kitchen again, Teresa sat down on a stool opposite Rita. "Don't think about what he said or what he did or even what your family thinks about all of this. There's just one thing to consider, Rita." She paused, shot her other daughter a don't-open-your-mouth look and asked Rita, "Do you love him?"

"Of course I love him, Mom. That's not the point."

"It's the only point," her mother said.

Gina kept quiet for as long as she could, then blurted out, "For God's sake, Rita, *all* men are impossible to deal with—"

"We can hear you!" their father shouted from the front.

Rita chuckled and shook her head. The heck with peace and quiet. *This* is just what she had needed.

"Am I wrong?" Gina shouted to her father. Then turning back to her mother and sister, she demanded, "See? Brothers, fathers, husbands, sons, they're all crazy. But giving up is never the answer, Rita. You have to dig in and fight back. Never give an inch."

"Your sister's right." Teresa nodded.

"It's a miracle!" Gina looked up at the ceiling to Heaven beyond and got a dark look from Teresa for her trouble.

Then, ignoring one daughter, Teresa reached out and took both of Rita's hands in hers. "I'm ashamed that you didn't fight for what you want, for what you need. Rita, we didn't raise you to walk away."

Her heart gave a sharp tug at the realization that that's exactly what she had done. In her own hurt and grief, she'd tucked tail and run away. But how could she not have?

"So I'm supposed to stay with a man who doesn't want me there?"

Gina opened her mouth and shut it again when her mother held up one hand.

"He does want you there. He told you so," Teresa said. "He wants you to leave before he loves you? What kind of statement is that? He already loves you and it scares him."

Rita laughed shortly and shook her head, denying the possibility. "Nothing scares Jack."

Although, the minute those words left her mouth she remembered Jack saying "You terrify me." Maybe her mother was on to something.

"Oh, honey," her mother said, "nothing scares a man more than *love* when it finally shows up." She gave Rita's hands a pat, then picked up a cookie and took a bite. "It's especially difficult for a strong man, because being out of control is a hard thing to accept."

"Jimmy wasn't scared," Gina muttered.

"Sure he was," her mother said on a laugh. "You just didn't give him time to think about it."

Shrugging, Gina admitted with a grin, "Okay, fair point."

"And your brothers?" Teresa laughed. "They were terrified."

"We can *still* hear you," Marco yelled.

Ignoring her son, Teresa looked at Rita. "Even your dad fought tooth and nail to keep from loving me."

"As if I stood a chance at that," Nick called out.

"Why do we have a door," Teresa wondered, "when everyone hears everything anyway?" Shaking her head again, she continued, "What I'm saying is, everything worth having, is worth fighting for."

Rita just didn't know. She'd left the penthouse in a rush, hurt beyond belief, angry beyond anything she'd ever experienced before. Heart aching, she'd had only one thought. Come home. To the family that was always there for her.

"So what're you going to do?" Gina spread a cinnamon-and-sugar mixture on the rectangle of dough then carefully rolled it up for slicing and baking. "You going to stay here? Or go back and reclaim your life?"

Well, that was the question, wasn't it? Being here with her family, she was starting to think and as she did, she was embarrassed to admit that running away from her problems, from the man she loved, just didn't feel right. She'd pulled back from him and hid away—the very thing she'd accused Jack of doing.

"Why should I leave?" she murmured, hardly realizing she was speaking aloud.

"Exactly," Gina agreed, slicing cookies and laying them on sheets to bake.

"I have a business there. And a home—okay, not the penthouse, but I was happy there and I can be again." Rita ate another cookie while her brain raced and the pain in her heart began to ease.

"Sure you can," her mother said.

"Jack doesn't make decisions for me."

"'Course not," Gina agreed.

"He doesn't get to tell me when to go. When to stay. Sit. Heel."

"That's my girl," Teresa cheered.

"Why should I make this easy on Jack?" Rita demanded of no one in particular.

"You never made it easy on any of us," Marco quipped when he brought an empty tray into the kitchen.

"Oh, please," Gina sneered. "And you were the angel child? Do you remember shaving my Barbie dolls bald?"

"A fond memory," Marco assured her, dodging when she took a swing at him.

"I'm going back," Rita announced. "And I'm going to look Jack in the eye and tell him that he can't dictate my life."

"I feel like I should have pom-poms," Gina murmured.

"He's not chasing me away," Rita proclaimed, scooting off the stool to stand on her own two feet. "I'm going back. I'm going to tell him he's in love with me and when he's done being scared of it, he can come and find me. I'm building a life there and I'm not giving it up."

"Good for you." Her father came into the kitchen and gave her a quick hug before grabbing another cookie. "But you can stay for a couple of days, right? Have a nice visit before you go back?"

"I sure can, Daddy," she said and leaned in to the most wonderful man she'd ever known. "Let Jack miss me. It'll be good for him."

"You women are devious, wonderful creatures," her father said.

"And don't you forget it," his wife warned.

Solitude was overrated.

Three days of it and Jack felt like he was suffocating. Quiet. Too much damn quiet. He kept seeing Rita's ghost in the penthouse. He heard her laugh. He caught her scent in the guest room she'd used and ached for her in a way he wouldn't have thought possible.

It was worse somehow, knowing that she was

in Utah. Jack hadn't really believed Cass when she told him that Rita had left the damn state. So he'd driven to Seal Beach, walked past the bakery and got a chill when he saw the closed sign on the door.

He'd driven her off and she'd actually left. He should be happy. Instead, he felt…hollowed out. Like a shell of the man he used to be. At that thought, he imagined what Rita would say to it and he could almost hear her. *Whose fault is that, Jack? Who keeps running away from life?*

Shaking his head free of irritating thoughts and reminders of all he'd lost, Jack turned his attention back to the stack of papers waiting for his signature. He'd been spending more time than usual in the office because it beat the hell out of being alone in the penthouse with too many memories.

"I'll get over it. Hell," he murmured, scrawling his name along the bottom of a contract, "*she'll* get over it."

"Mr. Buchanan?" Linda stood just inside the open door to his office.

"What is it?"

"Marketing reports *The Sea Queen* is now sold-out."

"Good. Great." The cruise liner would be a huge success, one more feather in the Buchanan family cap and Jack couldn't have cared less. "Is there anything else?"

"Just one thing." Linda stepped back, a smirk on her face and Rita sailed past her into the room.

The door closed behind her, but Jack hardly noticed. All he could see was her. That amazing hair of hers was a tumble of dark curls. Her eyes were sizzling. She wore black slacks, a lime-green shirt that clung to the mound of her belly and a white linen jacket over the shirt. Black sandals were on her feet and her toenails were a bright purple.

He'd never seen anything more gorgeous in his life.

Standing up behind his desk, he curbed the urge to go to her and grab hold of her. He'd done the right thing and he wasn't going to backtrack now. "Rita. I thought you were in Utah."

She tipped her head to one side and gave him a cool glare. "Hoping I'd stay so far away you'd never have to think about me again?"

"No." There was nothing on this earth that could keep him from thinking about her. "I just—"

"I didn't come to chat, Jack," she said, cutting him off as she dug into the oversize black tote slung over her shoulder. She pulled out a large manila envelope and handed it to him.

"What's this?"

"It's an ultrasound picture of your daughter."

His eyes widened, his jaw dropped and his fingers tightened on the envelope. "I thought you didn't want to know what the baby is."

"Turns out," she said, "surprises aren't as much fun as I used to think they were."

Okay, he knew that was a dig for the way he'd ended things between them. And fine, she was due a fair share of hits. He could take it. Then what she'd said suddenly hit him.

"A daughter?"

"Yes," she said, and clutched her fingers around the handle of her bag. "It's a girl. And I wanted you to know."

"Thanks for that…"

"I didn't do it to be nice, Jack," she said, interrupting him. "I came here to tell you that I'm not running away. I'm not *you*. I don't hide."

"I'm not hiding."

"Call it whatever you want to," she said, voice tight. "It amounts to the same thing."

Sunlight spilled into the office through the wide windows, lying in long, golden rectangles across the floor. Rita stood in one of those slices of light and it was as if she were glowing from the inside. Even the ends of her hair shone, and the sunlight was reflected in her whiskey eyes, making them look as if they were on fire.

"You're upset, I know," he started.

"Damn right I'm upset, Jack." She stopped, took a long breath and steadied herself. "But I didn't come here to get into another futile argument, either."

Still holding the envelope he wanted very badly to open, he asked, "Why are you here, then?"

"To tell you that I'm staying. Our daughter will be raised by *me*, in the apartment over the bakery. I'll tell her all about you, but you're not going to be a part of our lives, Jack."

"You can't keep her from me."

"Watch me," Rita countered. "You don't want *her* or me. You just want to do what you think is the 'right' thing. Well, I don't care about that. My daughter's going to grow up loved. Happy. And if her father isn't willing to give up his self-pity party long enough to be grateful to be alive, then he just won't be a part of our lives."

"Self-pity?" He repeated the words because they'd slapped him hard enough to make an impact. Was that who he was? Who he'd become? Was she right? "That's what you think?"

"Jack," she sighed out his name. "If you ever manage to work your way out of that cocoon you've wrapped yourself in long enough to realize you love me, let me know. Until then? Goodbye, Jack."

He looked up as Rita turned around, stormed across the room and out the door, slamming it behind her.

Jack fell asleep that night, still holding the ultrasound picture he couldn't get out of his head. A daughter. A little girl. Torn between desire and caution, he wasn't sure which move to make. And then the dream came.

It was hot. So hot every breath seared his lungs. He squinted into the too-bright sunlight and signaled to his men for quiet as they approached the village.

Shots were fired. Explosions rocked all around them, making his ears ring. Someone screamed and another shot fired and Jack was down. Pain burst in a hot ball in the center of his chest. Air caught in his lungs, refusing to move in or out. Jack stared up at a brassy sky, the sun beating down mercilessly and he knew he was dying.

But this wasn't how it happened. The dream was wrong.

Then Kevin was there, leaning over him. Jack looked up at his friend. "I'm hit. I'm hit bad."

"Yeah, dude. It doesn't look good."

"But this is wrong. You were wounded, not me." Jack breathed past the pain, felt it sliding through his body. "Help me, Kev. Do something. I did it for you."

"Yeah, you did." Kevin grinned and was suddenly in a wheelchair. "And I appreciate it. Wish I could help you now, bro. But it's all on you."

None of this made sense. Jack looked around. The sand. The sun. The men. Everything was the way it always was in his dream. Well, except for Kevin, grinning like a moron at him from a chair.

"What's so funny? Do something, damn it!"

"Nothing I can do, dude," Kevin assured him. "It's a heart shot. You're done for. There's no hope."

Panic roared through him followed by fury. Damned if he'd end like this. "What the hell kind of help is that? Call a medic. Slap a bandage on my chest."

"Hearts can't be healed with a damn bandage, man. You're way past that."

Fear and fury were a tangled knot inside him. "Then what do I do?"

"You already know that, Jack," Kevin said. "You're not shot, man. Your heart's broken and the only way to fix it is to find Rita and make this right. It's as good as over for you."

Reaching down, he held out one hand and waited for Jack to take it. Then Kevin pulled him to his feet and slapped Jack on the back. "The only way out is Rita."

"Rita." Jack looked down at his chest. He wasn't bleeding. He was healthy enough. He was just...lost. Lifting his head, he glanced around. The dream had changed. The desert was gone.

He was on the beach, the roar of the sea pounding in his brain. And there was Rita, standing at the shoreline as she had been on the first night he'd seen her. And just like that, Jack knew Kevin was right. He felt as if his heart had been ripped out of his chest. It was over for him.

It had been over from the first moment he'd seen her.

Just the memory of her was strong enough to tear down the dream that had been haunting him for months. Rita had drawn him out, with the help of an old friend.

But when he turned to thank Kevin, the man was gone. Looking back down the beach, he saw Rita, holding a baby girl with dark brown curls and bright eyes. He started toward them just as Rita smiled. Then slowly, she and the baby faded until they finally disappeared completely. When he stood alone on the darkened beach, pain hit him like a fist.

Fix this, *he told himself,* or lose everything.

Jack woke with a start and sat straight up in bed. His mind racing, heart pounding, he realized so many truths at once, he was breathless. Maybe it made sense that the lesson he needed to learn had come from Kevin. He'd think about that later. Right now, he knew what he had to do, so he lunged for his cell phone on the bedside table.

He punched in a familiar number and waited interminably as it rang on the other end.

"Dad? Yeah, it's me, Jack." He walked out onto the terrace, into the teeth of the wind and had never felt warmer in his life.

"Jack? Are you all right?" his father asked. "What time is it?"

He winced and glanced at the clock. Two o'clock. He rubbed his eyes and laughed shortly. Taking a deep breath, Jack realized that for the first time in months, he didn't have a cold stone in his belly. In fact, he felt pretty good.

"Weirdly enough," he said, "I think I am all right. Or I will be. I'm sorry it's so late, but look. I need you to do something for me."

Eleven

"So have you thought of a name for her yet?"

Rita looked at her bakery manager and shook her head. "No, but I have plenty of time."

"Yeah, you do. But just remember, Casey's a great name for a girl."

Laughing, Rita slid the tray of cookies into the oven. It was good to be home. She'd needed that visit to her family, but being here was what felt right. Back in her apartment over the bakery, doing familiar work with people she loved, it was all good.

Sure, she missed Jack desperately, and there

was an ache around her heart that she was really afraid would be permanent. But she would learn to live with it. Learn to live without him, because she had to.

"Thanks, Casey, I'll keep that in mind."

When her phone rang, Rita answered, still laughing. "Hello?"

"Rita, this is Thomas."

Jack's father? For a second a thread of fear wound through her. Was Jack okay? Had something happened? Would she always be wondering about him? The answer was of course, yes.

Sighing, she said, "Hi, Thomas, everything all right?"

"Oh, yes, yes. Everything is great, really. I was just wondering, though, if you might do an old man a favor."

Setting the timer on the oven, Rita wandered to the refrigerator and pulled out a bottle of water. She uncapped it, took a long drink and said, "Of course. What can I do?"

She heard the smile in his voice when he said,

"I hoped you could come down to *The Sea Queen* to see me."

"You're on the ship?"

"Yes," he said. "I'm taking the first cruise. Thought I'd get a little golf in on the islands. But there's something I'd like to give you before I go."

Rita did some fast thinking. She really liked Jack's father and just because the man's son was behaving like a loon didn't mean she couldn't be close to his family. Thomas was, after all, her daughter's grandfather. And Jack's sister was going to be the baby's doctor. Family mattered, whether Jack could see that or not. "Of course I can. What time do you want me there?"

"Wonderful," he said, pleasure ringing in his voice. "As for what time, the sooner the better."

Now she was curious. Jack hadn't said anything to her about his dad going on the first cruise. But then, she told herself, maybe he didn't know. What could Thomas possibly have to give her that was important enough for her to go scurrying down to the harbor just before the ship sailed?

"Okay, I'll just arrange for my manager to take over and I'll come right down."

"Thank you, Rita. I'll leave word at the dock and they'll bring you to my suite."

"Okay, then," she said, still baffled, "I'll see you soon."

She hung up and just stared at the phone for a second or two. Rita had no idea what was going on, but the sooner she got to the harbor, the quicker she'd find out.

Half an hour later, she was boarding the ship and being met by a young man in a navy shirt and sharply creased white slacks. *The Sea Queen* was stitched onto the breast pocket of his shirt and just below, he wore a name tag that read "Darren."

"Mrs. Buchanan?" he asked and when she nodded, he said, "If you'll come with me, Mr. Buchanan is waiting in the owner's suite."

The crowds were frantic. People rushing around, having their pictures taken, waving to people on the dock. Children ran past her, their laughter hanging in their wake. The scent of the sea flavored the air and Rita lifted her face into the wind briefly before boarding an elevator with Darren.

"Everyone seems really excited," she said.

"They are," Darren assured her. "It's a great ship and it's always fun to go out on the first cruise."

Probably would be, she thought and told herself that one day she'd have to try it. Right now, sitting on an island beach with nothing to do sounded pretty good.

She had no idea what deck they were on when the elevator stopped and they stepped off into a luxurious hallway. But it was quiet with none of the eager abandon down on the main decks. Darren led her to a door at the end of the hall, then opened it for her.

"Mr. Buchanan said you should just go on inside, ma'am," he said, then strode quickly away, back to the elevator.

Rita walked into the massive suite, closed the door behind her and for a second, all she could do was stare with her mouth open. It was more than elegant. It was opulent.

Midnight blue carpeting was so plush her feet sank into it. There was a huge living area, with a flat-screen TV, an electric fireplace and several couches and chairs all done in cream-colored fabric. There was a bar, and out on the private balcony, she could see a table and chairs as well as lounges.

She'd love to get a look at the rest of the suite before she left, but for right now… "Thomas?"

Someone stepped into the room from the terrace, but it wasn't Thomas. Even before he spoke, she knew it was Jack because her blood started bubbling and her heart leaped into a gallop.

"Thanks for coming, Rita," Jack said.

She backed up. Cowardly, yes; she'd be embarrassed later. "What're you doing here? Where's your father?"

"That's the thing. He's not here. I asked him to call you for me, since I figured you wouldn't speak to me anyway."

"You were right about that," she snapped and turned for the door. She had to get out of there. Off the ship, back to the bakery.

But Jack was too fast and his legs were much

longer than hers. He beat her to the door and stood with his back against it, blocking her way.

"Move, Jack."

"Not yet."

"You really don't want to push me right now," she warned, though she didn't know what she could do to move him if he didn't want to be moved. Gina would kick him, but Rita just wasn't the kicking kind. Too bad.

"Just hear me out. Then if you want to leave, I won't stop you."

"Why should I?"

One corner of his mouth quirked up and her heart thudded painfully in her chest. "Because you're curious. Admit it."

She hated that he was right. Hated that he could make her body burn with a half smile and hated that just standing this close to him made her want to lean in and take a bite of his lower lip. "Fine. Talk."

He shook his head. "Not here. Come in. Sit down."

When he took her arm, she pulled free of his grasp. She didn't trust herself to stay mad if he was touching her and she really wanted to stay mad. She'd earned it, hadn't she?

"No," she said. "I'm not sitting down. I'm not staying. Just say whatever it is you want said and get it over with." She felt a little wobbly. Too many emotions churning inside at the same time. Didn't he know how hard this was for her? Didn't he care at all? Shaking her hair back, she said, "Unless you've brought me here to declare undying love, then just let me go, okay?"

"That's why you're here," he said softly.

"What?" She couldn't have heard him right, Rita told herself. Jack wouldn't have said that unless he had another agenda. "What're you saying, Jack?"

"I love you."

She swayed in place and he instinctively reached out one hand to steady her. Tears blurring her vision, Rita slapped at his hand. "No, you don't. You're just telling me what you think I want to hear."

Irritation bloomed on his face. "I should have known you wouldn't react the way I expected you to. You've always surprised me, so why should now be any different?"

"What are you talking about?"

"I'm trying to tell you that I was wrong. That I love you. That I want you—but if you're not going to believe me why bother?"

"I didn't say I didn't believe you—" She broke off, stared up into his eyes and saw, along with sparks of exasperation, the love she'd always hoped to see. "You love me?"

"Now will you sit down?" he asked.

"I think I have to," she said. She was shaking all over and her heart was pounding so quickly it sounded like a frantic drumbeat in her ears.

Once she was perched on the couch, Jack started pacing. He glanced at her and said, "You were right."

"Always a good start," she said. "Right about what?"

"Pretty much everything." He paced away from her, then whirled around and came back. "I was hiding. Not just from pain, but from life. I didn't really see that despite how many of you kept trying to tell me. I guess it's not easy for a man to admit he's been a damn coward."

"I didn't say you were a coward."

"No," he agreed, "that's one thing you didn't say. But it's true anyway. Hell, Rita, seeing Kevin again, it shook me. Then the wedding, him and Lisa, you and me… It was like an overload or something. My brain just exploded."

"So you told me to leave."

"It seemed like the right thing to do at the time—"

She started to speak but he cut her off for a change.

"—but it wasn't. Damn it Rita, I've *missed* you. Your voice, your scent, the taste of you. Hell, I miss that loud laugh of yours so much I keep thinking I hear it echo around me."

"Loud?" she repeated.

He grinned. "Loud. And sexy as hell."

Rita took a breath and held it, really hoping this was going to keep going the way she wanted it to.

"That day in the desert almost finished me and did a hell of a lot more to Kevin." Jack stopped pacing, stared into her eyes and said, "But he got past it. Moved the hell on, found a life, while I was still stuck in the past, trying to rewrite history."

"Oh, Jack." She was glad to hear that he had done some thinking, but she hated hearing him put himself down like this, too. It was, she thought, the way of family. *I can call my sister names but if you do it, we go to war.* Well, that's how she felt here, too.

"Just let me get all of this out, okay?" He pushed one hand through his hair. "I've been doing a lot of thinking the last few days and last night, it all sort of came together."

"How?" She needed to know. Needed to believe that this was all real and that somehow he wouldn't go back down that dark road he'd been so determined to stay on.

"The dream came again."

And she hadn't been there to help him through it. Pain for what he'd been through chimed inside her as she pushed off the couch to go to him. "Jack…"

"No," he said, smiling. "It wasn't the same at all this time. In lots of ways. And it doesn't matter right now. All that *does* matter is that I finally figured something out."

She looked up into his eyes and for the first time, noticed that he seemed different somehow. There weren't as many shadows in his eyes. He looked…lighter. As if at least a part of the burden he carried with him had slipped off. And that gave her hope.

"What, Jack? What did you figure out?"

"That I was an idiot. Telling you to go when I should have been begging you to stay." His gaze moved over her face like a touch. "Hell, Rita, I should have been thanking the Fates for bringing you back to me and instead, all I could think about was if I loved you and lost you it would kill me."

Tears blurred her vision but she blinked them back. She didn't want to miss a moment of this. "So," she said wryly, "to keep from losing me, you lost me."

"Yeah." He sighed. "Like I said. Idiot."

"Agreed."

He laughed shortly. "Well, thanks."

"Hey, who knows you better than me?" She asked and reached up to smooth his hair back from his forehead.

"Nobody," he said, voice hardly more than a whisper. He laid both hands on her shoulders and stared directly into her eyes when he said, "Forgive me, Rita. I was too messed up to see what I had. What I lost. I told you once that you had to leave before I loved you."

"Yeah," she said, the memory of that pain filling her. "I remember."

"That was a lie, too." He rested his forehead against hers. "I loved you the minute I saw you on that beach. When you smiled at me, my heart dropped at your feet. I didn't want to acknowledge it and that's the idiot part." He slid his hands up to cup her face and wiped away a single tear with his thumb. "But my heart is yours, Rita. Always has been. I love you."

She sucked in a gulp of air and held it. "Say it again."

He grinned. "I love you. More than I ever thought possible to love anyone."

"Jack…"

He frowned a little. "Is that an irritated sigh, or a dreamy one?"

Rita smiled up at him. "Dreamy. With just a little bit of irritation tacked on to the end for what you put us all through."

"That's fair," he said, nodding. "Rita, I want to stay married to you. I want to raise our daughter and however many more kids we have together. I love you. Always will. I'm sorry I hurt you. Sorry I hurt my family. My friends."

She reached up to cover his hands with hers. "I love you, Jack."

"Thank God." He sighed in relief. "You'll never be sorry, Rita. I swear it."

"I never was sorry, you dummy," she said and went up on her toes to kiss him.

Jack took her mouth like a drowning man taking his first clear breath. She leaned in to him, wrapped her arms around his neck and held on as he picked her up and swung her in a circle, their mouths still fused together.

Finally though, breathless, he broke off and grinned down at her. "I love you."

"Keep saying it," Rita told him. "I want to hear it. A lot. In fact, I'm going to send Kevin and Lisa a thank-you card for inviting us to their wedding."

"Oh!" Jack let her go long enough to walk to a table, pick something up and come back to her. "Hey, that reminds me. I brought this along for you to see. Kevin sent me an email this morning. I learned my lesson there, too, and opened it right away. Then I printed it."

Rita's eyes blurred again as she looked down at the picture of Kevin and Lisa, standing side by side. The picture was captioned "Got my new legs. I'm an inch taller than I used to be. Thanks again, Jack. For everything. Give us a call sometime."

She looked up at Jack. "That's so great."

"Yeah, it is." He took the picture, tossed it to the table again, then held her hands in his. "And one of these days, I'll thank him for waking me the hell up in time to save the only thing that matters to me." He cupped her cheek with one hand. "You, Rita. I love you."

"I love you back," she said and felt her world completely right itself and steady out. He'd been worth the fight. Worth the pain. Worth everything to get to where they were now.

Bending down, he kissed her baby belly and then stood up to face her. "You know I told you I've been doing a lot of thinking the last couple of days and I wanted to ask you something. How do you feel about naming our daughter Carla? After my mom."

Rita's heart melted. It was perfect. It was all so perfect. She stepped into his embrace. "I think I love it. You're back, Jack. Really back, aren't you?"

"Yeah." He gave her a smile. "I'm finally home. *You're* my home, Rita. I know that now." His arms closed around her and she felt the steady thump of his heart beneath her ear. She had Jack. She had her daughter. She had everything.

The ship's horn sounded and Rita jumped. "Hey, we've got to get off the ship before it sails."

He only tightened his hold on her and laughed. "No, we're not getting off."

Confused, she stared up at him. "What do you mean?"

"Just in case you didn't kill me," Jack said, grinning, "I arranged for Gina to come to town to run the bakery for two weeks. My dad's coming out of retirement to run the company and you and I are sailing to St. Thomas."

"You can't be serious," she whispered, a little panicked, a little excited.

"Absolutely serious."

"But, I don't have any clothes…"

"We'll buy whatever we need." Then he kissed her and admitted, "But I'll say I'm going to want you naked most of the time."

Oh, boy. A tingle of anticipation set up shop low down inside her. But could she really just leave? On the spur of the moment?

"But—" Was this happening? When she woke up that morning, she'd been alone and afraid she would stay that way. Now, she had Jack, a dream vacation and the life she'd always wanted being handed to her. How could she keep up?

"Oh," he said, that tempting smile curving his mouth again, "Gina said to tell you she had lots of ideas on how to 'fix' your bakery."

Rita's eyes narrowed on him. "Oh, you're going to pay for that," she promised.

"Can't wait," Jack said and bent to kiss her again. "You brought me back to the world, Rita. Let me show you some of it."

And just like that, it was all right. She'd go with him anywhere.

"Show me, Jack. Show me everything." Love shone so brightly all around them it was blinding, and Rita would never stop thanking whatever Fates had brought them back together.

"Come with me," he said and dropped one arm around her shoulders, pulling her in close to his side as he led her out to the balcony. And there they stood, wrapped in each other's arms, looking ahead as they sailed into the future. Together.

* * * * *